Pearly Scott

The Magicians of Galway

*Reveal the secrets only to those
who will understand*

Pearly Scott

The Magicians of Galway

MERANO-VERLAG

Bibliographic information from the German National Library:
The German National Library lists this publication in the
German National Bibliography; detailed bibliographical data
can be found on the Internet at http://dnb.dnb.de.

Production: BoD - Books on Demand, Norderstedt

Bibliografische Information der Deutschen Nationalbibliothek:
Die Deutsche Nationalbibliothek verzeichnet diese Publikation
in der Deutschen Nationalbibliografie; detaillierte
bibliografische Daten sind im Internet über dnb.dnb.de
abrufbar.

© 13/07/2020 – Merano-Verlag

Herstellung:
BoD - Books on Demand, Norderstedt

ISBN-13: 978-3-944700-13-7

Inhalt:

1473 – The great fire of Galway.....................7

Karma...........................21

The Power of Light.....................27

Ghosts of the Dead.....................35

1477 – Colombo.....................41

Indian Insights.....................53

Callahan's Wrath.....................59

From Fairies and Elves.....................65

Callahan's Legacy.....................71

The Cave.....................83

Reflections.....................97

Revenge.....................107

Orla.....................115

About the book and how it was created.....................117

*We carry
the true treasures
in ourselves

-

forever.*

1473 – The great fire of Galway

The flash went down from the sky with a huge thunder on this beautiful spring day in the landscape of Galway, in Ireland. Aiden got hit by the first huge raindrops and he knew, he had to take cover quickly if he wanted to prevent to get wet to the bone. So, he ran to a small cottage made of wood and stones taken from the surrounding fields and with a roof made of straw.

He was freezing as the cold wind blew through the holes of the open windows, which had no glass in it. At least he was protected from the bad weather somehow and he looked at the dark clouds, moving fast in the sky.

Aiden had no fear as he was used to the Irish weather, but he was quite surprised by this sudden change today. Normally weather did not get rough so quickly. Something was not as always. The sky looked terribly angry today and the lightning was awfully close and dangerous.

For now, Aiden had escaped and felt safe. He enjoyed being in the nature, feeling the wind on his skin and the raindrops in his face. As he looked through one of the window holes to watch the clouds quickly moving forward, he heard a sound behind himself.

There was a huge man standing in the open doorway, with a black long coat, wet from the heavy rain and with a dark hat, that threw a shadow on the man's face.

"What are you doing in my cabin? Out with you! Out!" shouted the man in an unfriendly way, as he grabbed Aiden on his shirt in the neck. He forced Aiden outside the cottage with a push, back into the heavy rain. Now Aiden knew, this was Callahan, the mayor of Galway and so-called "land protector".

Aiden decided to run homewards to get not more rain than necessary. He would be wet and cold overall when he would arrive at home, that was certain by now. Aiden did not like

Callahan as this man was always unfriendly to everyone. But what could he do? He had to accept the situation and run as fast as he could to reach his home, getting back into a warm and dry environment.

When Aiden reached the family's house, he entered quickly and closed the door behind himself. Water ran down his clothes building a large puddle on the floor.

"Aiden! Come in", said Teagan, his mother. "Put other clothes on, dry one's and come to the fire to warm you up. I would not want you to get a cold." Aiden's mother knew that it was impossible for the boy to escape that bad weather as it really came in too fast. She was worried about Aiden's safety, when he was out. Now, that he was finally back home, she felt relieved as she knew Aiden was now protected from rain and lightning of the thunderstorm.

"I was safe in a cottage when Callahan came and threw me out", Aiden complained.

"He is a ruthless idiot", Aiden's mother confirmed. "I don't like him either."

Aiden was sitting at the fireside and watched the flames consuming the wood, sparkling and crackling.

"Where is father?", Aiden asked his mother. "Isn't he back by now?"

"No, not yet. He should have arrived quite some hours ago", his mother replied. "I hope he has found some cover from that weather, somewhere."

Aiden hoped his father would return soon as it was his eleventh birthday today and he wanted to celebrate it with his parents, as soon as both would be at home.

The hours passed, the evening came, then the night laid down over Galway – but Aiden's father did not return.

Early morning, next day, Donal came by and knocked on the door to request entry. Donal was known to be a magician, he owned a huge area of land and was a very wealthy man. So, he could afford to establish a school in Galway, where he raised young talented girls to also become magicians. He was mysterious in some way, though he was always friendly and helpful to anyone, who came to him for help. But he also kept some secrets, which he would not reveal to everyone. That brought him suspicious thoughts from quite some people here in Galway. Donal did not care about this. He simply continued with his work and studies of the obscure sciences and ancient knowledge. His community of female magicians was also well respected for their ability to help cure the sick or give counsel to families when someone faced death, suddenly and unexpected or slowly in the course of a disease.

"Teagan, please sit down", Donal asked, while he was entering the tiny house.

"What is it?" Teagan wanted to know, as she slowly sat down in a chair. She was already somehow disturbed and had trembling fingers, as Aiden saw.

"It's about Owen", Donal said. Owen was Teagan's husband, the father of Aiden. "He did not return yesterday, as we had hoped and I have reason to believe, that he will not be able to come back to you. I am terribly sorry, but I assume", Donal took a deep breath, "he lost his life."

Teagan got tears in her eyes as she looked at Donal. She did not want to believe it, yet she knew, Donal would never lie or talk about such things easily.

"What happened?", she wanted to know.

"I can't say", Donal replied. "All I know is, that things did not run as expected and the information I received was not clear on what has happened exactly. So, I really cannot tell you more about it." Donal again took a deep breath. "All I can say and promise to you is, that you will get all kind of support, that you may need to get through this difficult situation and the community of the Galway magicians will support you, as good as we all can. And – we all hope to learn more about what really happened and if there is any hope to bring Owen back alive, if possible.”

Aiden, who listened carefully to Donal's words, cried silently. Tears were running down his cheeks, dropping on his shirt. He loved his father and he could not stand the thought, that he might never see him return.

“Thank you for your generous offer, Donal”, said Teagan. “And thank you very much for keeping me informed about Owen. I still do not want to believe, that Owen might have died. I will keep my hope and live in a sense, that Owen will return home, one day. Whenever that day might be.” She stood up, made a step towards Donal, laid her hand on Donal's shoulder and said: “It's really good to have you and your community around. You are great people and I really appreciate your doing – and your way to act on things. I don't know, how to thank you enough, Donal.” Teagan had more tears in her eyes. She was a strong woman and had a warm and generous heart, and she was deeply hit by the thought, Owen might be dead. And she also knew that she could not do anything about it for now.

“Would you like to stay with us, Donal, and celebrate Aiden's birthday with us? Yesterday, we waited so long and finally went to bed without a chance to have cakes and a present for Aiden”, Teagan invited Donal.

“Under these circumstances, Teagan, I am happy to join you”, Donal replied, and to Aiden he said: “Aiden, I would rather celebrate your birthday together with you and both your parents, believe me that, please. Now – as we cannot change the things being, let us make the best out of it and have a piece of cake to give your birthday at least the attention, it deserves. And believe me, my boy, I feel terribly sorry, that your father is not with us now.”

Teagan brought some plates with cake for Aiden, Donal and herself and some cups of tea for each of them. Then she brought a birthday present for Aiden and handed it over to him.

"This is your birthday present, Aiden. Your father and I – we decided, it is time for you, as you grew up already so fast, to give you this rare book. And we both hoped, you might like to use it with great care and pleasure."

Aiden was surprised and received the book out his mother's hands. "Thank you so much, mommy", he said thankfully. Then he started unpacking the book. As he saw the book's title, his mouth fell open. "Fire magic. How to evoke and control the power of fire entities", Aiden read.

Donal became bigger eyes, it seemed. "Teagan, please, do you really think, this is a good idea to have Aiden read such a book?" he asked, slightly disturbed.

"No, after what might have happened yesterday and with the fact, that Owen is missing, I don't think it is a good idea. But it was Owen's wish and I respect this. I just hand over, what was in his sense", Teagan replied.

"I have my concerns, really, Teagan. Please let me introduce Aiden to the power of magic and not let him do that by his own, without any guidance. You know, I would really like to take that task and do my supervision for Aiden", Donal proposed.

"No", Aiden said. "I don't want to be one of your female students. I would be the only boy among all these girls, and you cannot demand that from me. I am feeling unpleasant among girls. I don't like that idea, really", Aiden insisted. "I'd rather read the book and just in case I should have any problems with it, or would not understand the writings in it, I can come and ask for your help, sir", he said to Donal. "I really don't want to go to your school. Really not. Thank you for the offer, sir."

"Let's give Aiden the chance to read the book and maybe he comes to the conclusion that some help could be beneficial",

Teagan suggested. "Then we both would be very pleased to make use of your offer, Donal."

"As you wish", Donal replied. "Now, thank you very much for the cake, Teagan, it had a wonderful taste. As the sun is climbing up so quickly, I should return to the school now. And, Aiden – our doors will be kept open for you and it would be my pleasure to support your education to become one of the Galway magicians if you want. I know, it would be also in the interest of your beloved father, Aiden, and it would be my honor to assist with that."

As days passed by, Aiden continued to read in his birthday book about "Fire magic." The more he read, the more he got dragged into the topic. He was fascinated of the content and really tempted to do some practice, to see, if these incredible techniques could really work. He tried to focus his mind, as he had read in the book, to concentrate on the creation of a small fire entity.

Somehow, it did not work. Not even the slightest spark. Aiden felt a little bit disappointed and thought, maybe, he had not much talent for this magic.

He decided to use the sunny days to be out in the fields – that was one of his greater joys, and then, in the evenings, he would continue his reading and practicing.

One evening, as he walked over a meadow whose grass was damp from the dew, he saw him. Callahan. This unpleasant man came towards him, fast and determined.

"You again, lousy boy!" Callahan shouted from the distance towards Aiden. "This is my land, and I want you to get off of it! Piss off, now! Or I will throw you and your mother out of your house. Then you can live in a doghouse like shitty pigs!"

Aiden turned instantly and ran away. How he hated this dumb asshole! He ran and ran until he reached the family's house. He looked back and saw Callahan's field in the distance and the town of Galway behind the fields. Now his anger grew as the sun went down and darkness began to take ownership of the land.

Aiden went into the house and grabbed his book. He was more determined than ever before to try to practice and create some fire entities. Now he was in the mood to give all his will and might into the spellings, he had learned from the book.

Aiden stood with his hand held up into the dark sky as he concentrated to create a fireball. And – he could not believe it at first – here it was – his first tiny spark. Was that real? As soon as Aiden noticed his own surprise, the spark disappeared.

"Concentrate, focus, don't get disturbed, focus!", he told himself. Again – after some seconds, Aiden succeeded to create another tiny little spark. This time, he kept his conscious mind and focused constantly on the spark, as this grew slowly bigger, until Aiden saw a fireball in his hand. Then he noticed Callahan in the distance, walking towards Galway, where he lived.

Aiden felt his rage coming back like a wave, overwhelmingly pressing him into a state of fury. So, he called out loud "I hate you, Calla-ass!", and he threw the fireball towards Galway. Without hesitation, Aiden created a second fireball and did not even notice, how easy that was for him suddenly. Full of rage and anger he continued to throw the fireballs, one after the other, towards Galway, hoping he would succeed to hit Callahan's dumb head.

It was an amazing scene as all these fireballs flew through the dark sky and there was also great danger in the air. Wind came up and carried the fireballs right into the town of Galway where the roofs began to burn, quickly and with fast growing.

Galway was burning! The flames reached towards the infinitely high sky and the dark night was illuminated by a tremendous wave of flames.

Aiden did not even notice how frightened Callahan was, as he saw the happening. As he tried to understand, what was going on there, Callahan saw, that the fireballs came from the house, where Aiden lived with his mother, then he looked at Galway and had to realize, that almost every house in the town was a victim to the flames or at least severely threatened by the fire. Callahan ran towards his own house in Galway and he nearly died from a heart attack. He fell down, breathing heavily as he had challenged his fat and untrained body up to the limits. Callahan grabbed his chest as he thought, his heart was about to stop beating – then he lost consciousness and darkness took control over him.

As Aiden realized, what he had caused, he took his book and returned quickly into the house and went to bed. He did not say a word about all that. Somehow, he was a little bit proud of his act of revenge towards Callahan. He had shown this bloody asshole, what he deserved from being rude to Aiden. On the other hand, Aiden was frightened, that he might have caused huge damage to the homes of many innocent people. But hey – these dumb creatures had supported this ass to become the mayor of Galway. At least many of them accepted the situation. So, what? Aiden stopped thinking about all these happenings and more enjoyed his new ability to create fireballs out of concentration. What a wonderful new skill that might be, he thought!

Early in the morning a loud knocking at the door caused Aiden to wake up. What the hell! Was Callahan here to punish him for his fireworks now? Aiden was shaking and felt fear rising inside. How could he escape that situation? Should he simply deny or lie? Aiden was fully sensitive what would happen now.

Aiden's mother Teagan went to the door and opened it. Donal was outside, Aiden felt relieved.

"Teagan, have you already heard, what happened last night? There was a huge fire in Galway and many houses burnt to the ground", Donal explained.

"No, I have not heard about it yet", Teagan answered. "That is horrible."

"Yes, and the worst thing about it is, that Aiden had his part in it. He caused the fire to start as he played around with the fire magic and produced these fire entities, which burnt the town down."

"No, Donal, that cannot be true. Not my Aiden. You have to be wrong."

"I have nothing to do with it!", Aiden lied.

Donal looked at him intently, then said calmly but firmly: "Show me your hands, Aiden." When Aiden didn't respond, Donal took Aiden's right hand and showed it to his mother. There were clear burn blisters in the palm of the hand.

"Well - what is this, Aiden? Those are blisters that you got from the fireballs that you threw after Callahan in your anger, right?", Donal wanted to know.

Aiden's face flushed with shame. He breathed in and out heavily.

Teagan looked at Aiden and asked, "How did it happen, Aiden? Where did you get these bubbles from? Do you really have anything to do with the fire in Galway? I cannot believe it."

"Yes, it is true, mommy", Aiden admitted. "It was my fault. I did not mean to cause any harm, but I was so in rage as Callahan had insulted me deeply. I was so upset, that I simply lost control and used the fire magic for my revenge. I wanted to hit Callahan, not Galway, you must believe me."

"You are in big trouble, my boy", Donal said. "Callahan will come and search for you and then drag you to punishment for this. He saw, what you did."

Teagan was worried. "What can we do?", she asked Donal.

"It would be the best if I take Aiden with me to the school. On the one side, Callahan would not be able to lay hands on him, on the other side, Aiden could be taught, how to use his magic powers. If there is one thing, we all have learned from that happening, it is, that Aiden has a huge potential and talent, like his father. Only if we teach him right, we can make sure, that his talent and power flows in a good direction and only by that we can help prevent happenings like this huge fire blast we had yesterday in the town. I am certain this is the only way we have right now", Donal insisted.

"Oh Donal", said Teagan with a sigh.

"I don't want to go to the school, please", Aiden whined.

"You have to", Teagan replied. "It is the only way to keep you and the people around you safe. I do not like it either, but I do not see another way. I believe Donal is right and it is the best for you and for all of us, Aiden. We will not be so far apart and from time to time I might be able to visit you at the school, Aiden. But the most important thing right now is, to get you hidden from Callahan. Maybe – if he does not find you – he might forget about what happened. Maybe Donal can help us with that as well to wipe out Callahan's memory of last night."

"Yes, I think that is possible", Donal said. "But first, we must get the situation under control, and we may not want to get things out of line. Once we calm things down, we will have time to work out the best solution and maybe it is best to clean Callahan's memory, yes. But this must be well thought through. For now – Aiden – it is important, that you come with me. Right now, and as quickly as possible. So, grab your book and some personal things you need and follow me."

Aiden started to cry silently. Tears ran down his face as he once again tried to persuade his mother, not to let this happen: "Mommy, please. Help me, I do not want to go to the school. Can't we simply leave Galway forever?", Aiden suggested.

"Aiden, to run away is never the best solution. Make the best out of it, learn to use your talent and learn to prevent these kinds of happenings in the future. That is the most promising way. And please do accept the help Donal offers. He is a good friend of your father, since many years. I have full faith in Donal, and I trust his judgement, Aiden. You must be strong now. But it is as it is. You will go with Donal. He can and will protect you. And this is now my decision", Teagan said firmly.

Aiden continued to cry silently, and he wished he could disappear into a deep hole into the earth, or simply vanish into the air. But this was not his choice to make. For now, he had to conform to his fate and go with Donal. He grabbed his book and some clothes and fell into his mother's arms while tears were still running.

"Bye, mommy", he whispered silently.

"Bye, Aiden", Teagan replied.

Then Donal took Aiden's hand and guided him outside the house to take him to the school of the Galway magicians.

After a long walk from the house, where Aiden lived with his mother, Donal and Aiden reached the buildings of the school of the Magicians of Galway, which lied on a hill and was surrounded by walls, that gave protection to the people living in the school's area. Donal opened the heavy door, made of solid wood, and let Aiden walk inside, then he himself came in and closed the door again.

Inside the walls Donal walked to a building, that was in the center of this complex of houses. Donal again opened the door and invited Aiden to step in. Then he followed him inside this house. It was the main schoolhouse of the complex. Aiden saw a couple of women and girls inside and Donal introduced Aiden to them.

"This young boy is Aiden, the son of Owen and Teagan. I have invited him to join our school for his education and practice in the arts of magic. He is very talented, and I have great faith, that he will have a bright future as a magician and we all could benefit from his abilities, once he has learned to use his talent in a good way. Welcome him, he is now one of us", Donal said.

The women and girls came nearer to welcome Aiden and each of them was introduced to the boy by Donal.

"This is Cassidy", Donal said, as the first woman came and reached out her hand to welcome Aiden. "She is one of the most experienced magicians we have, and her healing skills are well known, even to the people in Galway. Whenever you should have a physical or mental problem, let her know. She has great wisdom, sees how things relate to each other and what causes pain and problems to humans. If you listen carefully to Cassidy, you can learn a lot about health and well-being. She will teach you the knowledge how to heal, Aiden."

Aiden shook Cassidy's hand carefully and felt very shy in the presence of this impressive woman.

Then the next woman was introduced to Aiden. She was obviously younger than Cassidy and of the same beauty. "This is Ide", Donal said. "She will teach you how to communicate with spiritual entities like fairies and elves. She can see these beautiful beings and talks with them, like they were one of us. You will also learn that from her. It may take time, but Ide is exceptionally talented in that area. You will surely find that interesting, I believe."

"Hello", said Aiden quietly, as he shook Ide's hand. Somehow, he felt amazingly comfortable in Ide's presence and he could not tell why.

"This is Bridget", introduced Donal the next woman coming near. "She communicates with spiritual beings, all kinds of spiritual entities and of course with ghosts, souls of dead people, if you want. Many people are afraid of what she can do and many people do not like the thought that someone can communicate with the dead, but I am certain, you will learn how beneficial this skill can be, Aiden."

Bridget seemed to be a little cooler than Ide, or maybe Aiden just felt it that way, as he was not comfortable with the thought, that she had contact with the dead. He found the idea somehow spooky.

"Now, this is Darcy", Donal continued his introduction. "She is a young student, as you are, Aiden."

"Hello Aiden", Darcy said as she came near. "I can teach you how you mess up things and how everything goes wrong. I have always bad luck with all I do. I don't know why, but somehow that is my talent."

Aiden was surprised how firm Darcy shook his hand. She seemed to be a strong young woman, quite friendly though.

"And finally,", Donal said, as the last young woman came near, "this is Ciara. As Darcy, she is also a student in our school."

Ciara's look was somehow penetrating, as she inspected Aiden and he felt a little bit uncomfortable in her presence.

After this introduction round all magicians and students went to the tables in the room, where food was already prepared for them to sit down, to eat, drink and talk. Aiden sat down and Darcy came near to sit by his side. She told him a lot of stories she had experienced and presented him quite some unbelievable happenings. Aiden did not really know, what he should talk with her as he was just a young boy and he did not believe that his stories of being out in the fields of Galway would be of any interest to anybody here. And he definitely did not want to talk about his experience with Callahan, the mayor of Galway. No, definitely not.

The next days, Aiden was introduced into a lot of activities, the community had to perform to keep things going on. He learned a lot about how to grow plants in the garden, how to wash clothes, how to prepare meal and how to wash the dishes. Nothing so far about magic. Sometimes Aiden thought he would never be introduced in the interesting things like the firepower that he already had experienced.

On the other hand, Aiden was quite content, because he had a room for himself, where he could rest and read in his book. Donal allowed him that, although he told him to be careful and not mess up everything with a fireball inside the school. Aiden was not sure, if Donal was serious or if he made a joke at him. At least, he did not find that very funny.

Time went by, Aiden was safely hidden inside the school from Callahan, who was told, that Aiden had disappeared from his mother and no one seemed to know where to.

The only thing that prepared Aiden for the art of magic were the regular meditation sessions he participated. There he learned how to calm his mind down, how to let his thoughts flow and how to control his mind. It was necessary and seemed important to Donal that Aiden should first learn the basics, before he would be introduced to those arts, that could lead him on a dark path, if his character were not built firmly first.

Karma

Today, it was Aiden's twelfth birthday and all magicians and students gathered around him in the morning, at breakfast time, at the tables in the central school building. They congratulated him, one after the other, and then, Aiden saw someone coming through the door. He was not sure, if he could believe this, but what he saw brought tears in his eyes. His mother, Teagan, came to visit him. Aiden felt his heart beating strongly up to his throat as he ran to his mother and fell into her arms.

"Happy birthday, Aiden", she said. "I am so glad to see you. How are you doing here? Is everything alright?"

"Yes, mommy", Aiden replied as tears ran down his cheeks. "Yes, everything is fine here. I miss my freedom to walk outside the school in the fields and, what is even worse, I missed you, mommy. Can you take me home, please?"

Donal was worried as he saw that the boy was not yet happy to be part of the community in the school. Although Aiden was diligent and participated in all kinds of work and activities, he always seemed to be a little bit sad here. But he also knew that the danger, that Callahan represented, was still outside the walls of the school. He could not let Aiden go, for his own sake.

"Aiden, that is not possible", his mother said. "I really miss you every day of my life, but it is inevitable that you stay here. It is for your protection and what is even more important – it is for your education. You may not yet realize the path, that lays in front of you, but one day, you will see, how important these steps, that you take now, are for you and others. Why don't you show me, how you live here? Donal told me, you have your own room and I would also like to visit the rest of the school and, more importantly, learn to know all your friends and companions here, Aiden."

"Yes, I will make you familiar with everyone here and show you everything. But first, let us have some breakfast, please", Aiden replied and invited his mother to sit down at the table.

It was a beautiful and enjoyable day for Aiden, and he spent quite some hours with his mother that day. They had a lot to talk about, as months had been passed since they had last met each other.

Next day, Donal came towards Aiden and told him: "Aiden, today we will have a kind of new form of education for you. I will introduce you to some particularly important knowledge today. And I ask from you, that you listen carefully, make your own thoughts about what you will hear from me and then, please – and that is the most important part of this education, Aiden, then – you should draw your own conclusions. Never simply believe, what I tell you, that is important. Try to understand everything, and find out for yourself, if it can be true. You should not just listen and learn to be able to reproduce, what I tell you. You should seek the answers to everything by yourself. It is important, that you keep an open mind. Remain skeptical and think carefully about all that I will tell you."

"Why should I not believe everything, that you tell me, sir?", Aiden asked surprised.

"Well", Donal continued, "it is important, that you learn to think about everything. Nothing on this earth is obvious, you will see that during your education, Aiden. There is not always a clear true and false, there is not always the one right way. It may become exceedingly difficult sometimes to find the right thing to do. And because of that, you need the ability to carefully weigh all the information you receive and to come to your own, very individual and very personal conclusion. You will build your own truth, by time. And this is important, as that will help you to keep track of your path once it becomes difficult. You need a clear mind, and a good understanding of as much as possible. And you will learn to not only use your head to find the right solution, but also to use your heart and your inner voice.”

“My inner voice is in my head, sir. I cannot see the difference”, Aiden said.

Donal smiled. “I know, why you believe that. You know, your body is like a cathedral, everything is combined to something holy and divine. Your body, your mind, your feelings, your soul, your spiritual parts, everything. And your head is the belfry. Here is the most noise. And because of that, you cannot hear your inner voice. Believe me, your inner voice is not in the head, it is in your belly.”

“Okay”, Aiden said surprised and skeptical.

“Now, what you should know is, that you are not only your body and brain. There is more to that. Let me ask a question. What makes you unique, what would you say is different for you, when you compare yourself to others?”, Donal asked.

“I am twelve years old, so I am the youngest here in the school”, Aiden replied proudly, as he thought he had found the right answer.

“No, that is not, what I believe. There are many boys in Galway with twelve years, so that does not make you unique. What else could it be then?”, Donal asked again.

Aiden took a deep breath. He thought he should take a moment to think a little bit more about a good answer, as he did not want to look like a complete idiot, when all his attempts would be false. “Unique, unique to me, compared with all the others. What is unique…”, Aiden thought loudly. “Ah – there is one thing, that is really unique for me, that makes me different from anyone else”, Aiden finally said.

“And what is that?”, Donal wanted to know.

“Well – I see myself from inside, while I see everyone else from outside. That is, what makes me different, that is, what makes myself unique to me”, Aiden explained.

"Yes, that is it, Aiden! That is a particularly good answer to me", Donal confirmed, "and, because of that, it is your unique responsibility to take special care for your actions, Aiden. Because, you see yourself from the inside, and so you are the one, that is in the center of your world, even in the center of your universe. Every responsibility for everything that happens in your life comes from within yourself", Donal said and made a break, to give Aiden a chance to think about it.

"Why would I be responsible for everything? That does not seem right to me. I am not responsible that Callahan is such a pain in the ass to me", Aiden said, and after a while he added: "I am responsible for the fire in Galway, yes, but how can I be responsible for the actions that Callahan does?"

"It is because of your karma, Aiden", Donal explained.

"What is that?", Aiden wanted to know.

"When you are born, and you see yourself from the inside, then you know, that this is you and not one of the others. It is you, the center of the universe, if you want. And then – every action, that you take, creates responsibility in relation to the others. So, if you hurt someone, karma asks for yourself to also be hurt. Everything you do for others or to others will then also happen to yourself. That is karma. And why is that so? It is, that you learn, how things are connected and how they relate to each other. Let me say it in a different way. We are born to live, to make experiences, to feel life, how it really is. So, if you help someone to feel joy, when you give a present to someone, for example, then it is only fair and natural, that you get credit for this good deed in the way, that you deserve to experience the same joy, that you have created for this someone. Okay?"

"That sounds more reasonable", Aiden admitted.

"Yes, and it works the other way round as well. So, if you hurt someone, if you hit someone or kill someone, if you rob someone or burn someone to death – you also earn credit for that. You also deserved for yourself the reward to experience, how it is to be hit or burnt to death. That is karma. It is the absolute fairness of the universe."

"But this is cruel! And not everyone, that kills someone else gets killed himself. That is simply not, how it works. It is wrong, that is clear to me. It is not true, sir!", Aiden insisted.

"Yes, you are right, Aiden. If you only look on your present life, it is, or it seems, unfair. Not everyone who murders someone else is also killed in return. Not every thief gets something stolen from himself. Only – that is just a part of the story. This life, that you have now, Aiden, is not your only life. And it is not your first life. It will also not be your last life. It is continuing. And so, it is for everyone else. And that is a secret, not everyone knows. But once, you know about it, you will realize, that it makes sense, to think about, what you want to deserve as a reward for your actions and also for your thoughts and feelings, Aiden." Donal made a short break and then he continued: "If you kill someone, you will also be killed. Maybe not in this present life, maybe in the next or in one of the next. You, and everyone else too, will get the rewards, that are deserved. If you do good, you get back good. If you do bad, you deserve bad. It is as simple as that. And once, you know that and take responsibility for your activities, you have great power about how this life and your coming lives will be rewarded by the divine rules of the universe, Aiden. And this is all for today. Think about it carefully – and should you have doubts, it is okay. During all your education here, you will more and more understand. Just keep an open mind. That is all I would like to ask from you, Aiden. The rest comes, as it will be time."

"Sir, that was an interesting talking today. I would like to thank you for that, and I will think about it truly. Now I would like to go to my room to reflect on what you have told me, sir", Aiden said, before he could leave the education session.

The next day Aiden asked Donal, referring to the karma topic: "There is one thing about karma, I do not understand, sir. When we are born, we have no memory of our past lives. How can it be, that we still carry responsibility for things we did in a past life, when we do not even remember them? What sense does that make? To me, that does not seem logical. Can you explain that to me, please?"

"Yes, I understand your point, Aiden", Donal started to explain. "When we are born, we cannot remember, what we did before in previous lives, that is true – more or less. However, we come with our unique and individual character when we are born. And this character is a mirror of all things, we have lived through in our previous lives. Although we do not remember these things, we carry the fruits of our development within our character, and that helps us continue our eternal journey based on what we have already learned. Through all those things we experience and learn, we build our unique knowledge, our unique feelings for specific situations, you can say. All together this builds our conscience. There are things we are afraid of, for example, if we have died by drowning in the water before, we may be afraid of the sea or we feel uncomfortable swimming in a lake. And as we keep an inner memory of our death experiences in form of fears, which we cannot explain, as an example, so we also keep the good memories, those things, that feel familiar and comfortable to us. So, for example, if we had already been a musician in a previous life, we may be born with a talent for music or a preference for it. Somewhere in us, we still carry the memory and fruits of our past lives. And as you are making progress in your education, Aiden, the day will come, when you will start to remember more and more of these hidden treasures you carry within yourself."

The Power of Light

Cassidy began to teach Aiden after his thirteenth birthday. Her task was to introduce him to the skills of healing people. The basic part for this was, once again, to perform some meditations that aimed specifically to initialize knowledge and inner wisdom for the healing activities. Besides that, Aiden learned the basics about the human body, where the organs are positioned in a body and what physical task each organ has. Also, the spiritual tasks of the organs were explained to Aiden. He learned that a human's feelings are placed in the heart, in the center of the body, as it is a central task. He learned that kidneys have a relation to partnership and as humans have two kidneys, that it is important that both are working together to get their tasks fulfilled. The liver's task is to clean the body from all kinds of poison, be it alcohol or toxins from plants or whatever else. Rage is also placed in the liver. Stomach and intestines must digest everything and filter out all useful things, even impressions we get from our life. The spine is the backbone of our life, it carries the weight of our body and of our mental engagements. Every organ has a physical and a metaphysical or mental task.

Although Cassidy was careful with all the explanations and a real good teacher, Aiden was not excited about all this stuff. He was often bored and had no real interest in diseases or the causes for it.

Nevertheless, as this part was important for Aiden's education, Cassidy continued with great empathy to transfer as much of her knowledge to Aiden as she could. And after these organ-related sessions, she started to teach Aiden to work with light to transfer healing energies to diseased or weakened organs.

In one of the meditations she guided Aiden in a way that he should imagine a ball of light. He had to sense the ball's energy in his mind with his hands, concentrate on the ball and then use it to let a part of his body receive the energy of it, to feel its effect. Aiden felt recovered after this meditation. On the other hand, he was not surprised as he had felt healthy before and he really was not interested much in that stuff.

He was attentive to everything he was taught from Cassidy, but not curious.

One day at the dinner table, Ciara proposed to Aiden, that he might use this energy against Callahan, as she had learned from some previous discussions with Aiden, that he still had a problem with the mayor. "If you use the ball, that you imagine, to bring healing energy to a person, you can also create a ball, that sucks out someone's energy to weaken or create a disease, Aiden", Ciara explained. "And as you have a problem with Callahan, you could easily try to punish him that way for every bad thing he ever did to you."

Aiden had no big chance to think about it as Darcy interrupted spontaneously: "You better do not even try that, Aiden. You should not use your healing knowledge to do anyone any harm. That is not, how it's meant to be!"

"Yes, but it's possible!", Ciara insisted. "And Callahan would deserve a little punishment!"

"Sure, that might be true", said Darcy, "but as we all know are those activities always combined with our own karma. If we do bad things, they come back to us and do us harm as well. I do not need that shit as I already have enough problems myself, so I would not recommend to anyone to try that dark path!"

Aiden listened carefully to the discussion of these two young ladies, who already had many more hours of education than himself. He could only learn from their experience and he was inspired of the idea, that there was even more potential in those skills, than he was taught by Cassidy. That caught his attention in some way.

In one of the next sessions with Cassidy, Aiden learned about the connections of spirit, soul and body. "Aiden, you should know, that we humans are not our body alone", Cassidy explained to him. "We are spiritual beings in a human body. So essentially, it is about the experience of our spiritual incarnation, that we get through our physical state in this human body. We come to life with a purpose to experience, what it means to live, to take part in a creative way, to make something with our life that gives us a sense, a reason, that gives back something to the creation, to make our life a worthy one. And it is about our soul. As we experience life, we have a lot of possibilities to do things wrong or in a bad way. Karma always guides us back to what matters really. If we do bad, we get back bad and then we have a chance to understand, what bad is. Finally, when we collected a lot of good and bad experiences, we would see, that life is about positivity, creation and love, rather than destructiveness, greed or hate. When we live a peaceful, loving and creating life, then that fulfills us with joy and a divine state of mind. And that is good for our soul. No matter, how hard our lives might be sometimes, when we get back to a positive ground, we get closer to what makes us happy. So – when we are on a good course, our soul is fine with it. When we do things wrong, against our purpose or against the needs of our soul, sickness and disease find a fertile soil to grow in us. And illness starts on the spiritual layer, then slowly sinks into the body and we feel it on the physical layer. Whenever we see a problem with the body's organs, that is a sign, that we have missed the spiritual signs and did not ask ourselves enough, if we are still on a good course for our soul. Now, when we have a physical problem, we have the chance to help remediate that on the spiritual layer. If we understand the reason of the sickness, the demand of our soul, if we are able to interpret the signs, then we have a chance to cure or heal the body and return to a healthy state. It is complex and it helps, if you seek to understand as good a possible the various connections, that might have caused the illness originally. Can you follow that, Aiden?"

"I don't know", Aiden admitted, "as that is so much information and I think I do not yet fully understand the topic. Perhaps, if you could give me some examples, please?"

"Yes, sure. Let us assume someone has a work to do, together with others. And, whatever he does, he always gets criticized, there is no single day, where he would get told, that he did good work. What do you think, will happen with this human?", Cassidy asked.

"I believe, as that is very unpleasant for this human every day, that a lot of unpleasant thoughts might come to him about his work, about the others, who work with him, about the bad relationship to them. With all that, he should have a lot of sorrow and will not be happy at all. I can imagine that he might lose his appetite or might get problems with his stomach, as it is hard to digest all the bad impressions of his life at work. Does that make sense?", Aiden asked.

"Yes. It does make sense to me", Cassidy agreed. "Another example might be, when a woman lives together with a man in a house, where she does the household, the cooking, every work that has to be done at home and the man comes back home in the evening and always complains about every possible thing. What do you think, happens with the woman, Aiden?"

"Well, that's another unpleasant situation. It is hard to feel happy or have joy, if you are always criticized, so I would assume, there might be sickness on the way, too. As she breathes the same air in the house as her man, she might get sick with her lungs as an indicator, that the soul is revolting against living together with such a bad man. Maybe, her task is to understand, that it is important, that she should not only work for such a bad man but should rather act for herself to lead a better life. As the kidneys are the organs of partnership, she might also get an organic problem there. And maybe, if she has problems to separate herself from that man, she might get problems with her bladder, as she is not able to let go", Aiden assumed.

"Yes, all that might happen, Aiden, very good thoughts of yours", Cassidy confirmed. "It is important to know, that if you have ten people with the same problem, you might experience ten different ways of sickness. That makes things complex and requires a good understanding from you to feel into each individual people's situation and the reaction of their souls. People might have specific family-weaknesses as well. Some families always have problems with lungs, others with knees or with hearts. That might bring different outcomes, where the soul shows, that something goes wrong. And besides that, it is always an individual path, people go, so the signs of sickness vary, even if you have similar situations or problems, that cause the disease. So it is important for you, Aiden, that you develop a sense for that complexity, for the individuality and maybe, that you find a way to connect to people's souls, to get your information directly from the source. That requires sensibility and empathy. And you can grow that in you through your meditation practice, Aiden. That is an extremely helpful way to set free your mental capabilities and to sharpen your senses for subtle signs."

"Yes, I have already noticed, that my meditations help me get more sensitive to things I had not noticed before in my life. Sometimes, I have the impression, that I feel or know, what other people feel. Or I sense it when someone lies to me. That is so strange and somehow extremely helpful to me. I usually do not tell people what I sense or know in those moments, but it helps myself to better understand situations with people. I find that remarkably interesting, overall", Aiden admitted.

In the coming days, Cassidy continued to teach Aiden. "Our next topic, which is closely related to human's health, is, that we will talk about nature. As you might imagine, Aiden, as humans, we are born into a world, that is in a natural harmony, since thousands of years. When this planet came to life, the first things, that developed out of the source material, have been the minerals, then first living organisms appeared. Plants grew and spread over the surface of this planet, in the water and outside of it. And, also in the water, first little organic organisms arrived, which developed into animals of all kinds, by time. Then the first humans came. So we see, we have not been here from the first days, but have arrived at a point in time, where nature had already taken care of all kinds of living beings on this planet for centuries, for thousands of years. And as you can imagine, Aiden, as nature continued to support life on this planet, everything was in a stable harmony with each other. And now comes the point. Whenever something goes wrong, nature tries to get it back into the line, into the harmony. It is known to us, that, if there is a human being with a disease, nature grows a plant to help this human being to recover. It is a rule, a natural rule, to get things back into harmony. So, let us say, someone has a problem with his bones, it is certain, that a plant, that helps to cure that problem is growing nearby, where this person lives. It is as simple as that. People should be attentive to what grows in their garden, I would say. Because – if there is a new physical problem, a new sickness, it is normal, that a new kind of plant will be found in the garden. If you know that, by time, you will learn, which plant is good for which disease. That is good for people, who do not have other means to learn about that. Once, you are able to communicate with plants, or let us say, with the entities, that are responsible for plants, like Devas for example, you can directly ask and receive all kinds of helpful information about any kind of plant, you are interested in. I am not sure, if you know about the library of Alexandria. It carried a lot of precious knowledge about all kinds of topics, that are of high interest to us humans. A huge fire burnt this library down to the ground. And people still believe that all the treasures in that library have been lost in the fire. And now, here is the point: All the information about plants, that humans have collected in thousands of years can never be lost, as the plants themselves carry this knowledge. It is just about to learn, how to ask for and receive this knowledge again. Once you can do that, nothing is lost. And this is part of what we do for those people, who do not have such a connection to Devas or plants", Cassidy explained. After a short break, she continued: "Now, as you know that, when there is a person with a specific disease, nature grows a specific plant nearby to cure the disease, you can understand, that and how nature cares to bring things always back into harmony and balance."

"Wow", Aiden said. He was really impressed as he liked to be in the nature, to walk through wet grass, to observe insects and other animals and all the living out there. And he never thought about the possibility, that there was even more sense or intelligence in nature, than he would ever have expected. He now felt even more connected to nature. And he felt a growing interest inside himself, to learn more about those secrets of plants and what good they could do. "When will I learn to talk with Devas, Cassidy?", Aiden wanted to know.

"Well, this will be part of your education, that you will get from Ide. She is the one who communicates with all kinds of entities in the nature and she will teach you, how to do that. You need to be patient, as it is not yet time for that, but it will be part of your learnings here, and it is an important one", Cassidy said.

At dinner, Aiden once again sat together at a table with Darcy and Ciara, and he told them about the topic of the plants, he had learned today from Cassidy.

"Yes, you know, Aiden", Ciara started, "that plants even can read your thoughts? If you threaten them or offend them, they can even die, only because of your thoughts."

"Why would someone kill plants, Ciara?", Darcy asked. "That is stupid and not nice!"

"If you hate someone, you can kill his plants – only with your thoughts. That is, what it is good for, you see?", Ciara replied. "My mother told me that. She has already killed a lot of plants in the garden of our neighbors. One wrong word of this stupid bitch over there and she has no salad anymore", Ciara said with a diabolic smile in her face.

"That is not funny!", Darcy replied. "I could say, your mother is a witch, a bad one – but I do not say that, as I do not want to insult you or her. But I cannot agree with such doing, anyway. It is disgusting to me."

Aiden thought about the idea to kill Callahan's plants and he caught himself to have a smile in his face, then he had to admit to himself, that Darcy was right. All he had already learned about karma would strongly recommend to never think of killing plants in someone's garden ever.

"I think, one should not hurt or kill plants, that help humans only. That would be like punishing the innocent for something, that was not done by them", Aiden commented.

"Ah, what do you know?", said Ciara and was sulky.

Ghosts of the Dead

With Aiden's fourteenth birthday, Bridget started to educate him contacting spiritual entities and how to communicate with ghosts of dead people. It was the next chapter in Aiden's path to become a magician and he felt a little bit uncomfortable by the thought to talk to the dead.

"As you already know, Aiden", Bridget started her explanations, "all beings on our planet earth have a physical body and spiritual bodies. The main spiritual body is commonly known as the soul or as the astral body. Some people see the ghosts when relatives have passed in their houses, for example. That is normally an apparition of the astral body of the person, that has died. We also have many different forms of ghosts or spiritual entities around us, that sometimes affect people as they may be the cause for some spooky happenings." After a short break, Bridget continued: "It is important for you to understand, Aiden, that all this is totally normal and natural. It is spooky to people that have no experience with ghosts or entities. If you have experience after some time, it is all natural and talking with a ghost is quite the same as if you communicate with a living person. You know, when someone dies, the astral body is released from the physical body. The persons consciousness is still there within the astral body. The person is now on a spiritual level, normally is no longer seen by the living, is not heard, can no longer communicate with them. If this person had a problem before it died, this might cause trouble, often in combination with confusion, when the personal death is not accepted or recognized properly. Those souls might not walk into the tunnel of light, that normally appears to bring the astral bodies back into their spiritual home world. If such persons stay as a ghost in this intermediate world, they can act spooky indeed. They can push people or things, just to make the living aware, that they are still here and somehow alive. But if the living do not understand, what's going on, and do not make attempts to communicate with the ghost, they get even more frustrated. That can lead to a state that some ghosts are here for centuries, causing quite some confusion among the living, while being confused themselves. These ghosts can really benefit from help they receive from people like us, Aiden. When we communicate with them, we can try to find out, where their problem lies and then can help to create a solution for their problem. If we succeed, these ghosts might be willing to step into the light and go home properly. Then, we have done them a great favor, and also to the living that have maybe suffered by the presence of such a ghost."

"Wow, that is weird", Aiden said surprised and interested, "and how do we do that? How can we talk to those ghosts?"

"The first step is, that you get yourself in a state like in a meditation. Calm your mind, calm your thoughts and then, ask the ghost politely for a talk. Consider the ghost, or whatever entity you might have there, just like a normal human being, with all its previous knowledge, with all its previous feelings, capabilities and limitations, of course. Talk to the ghost with a loving and understanding attitude. That will help most to create a good basis for your communication. And consider, please, and this is especially important, to always create a protection first, before you try to communicate. Protect yourself, Aiden", Bridget warned.

"How do I do that?", Aiden wanted to know.

"You create a ball of light around your body, no matter if you sit or stand, you imagine, that you are inside of a bubble of light. Best take violet light and imagine, that you are safe and protected by this bubble of light and that nothing can come through, that would cause you any harm or problems. Only good things can come through this bubble. If you have that in your mind, then you can start to talk to the ghost. And for that, it is fully sufficient if you think, what you want to communicate. You do not have to talk loudly, it is sufficient if you think, what you would like to say or ask. Every ghost is enabled to read your mind – if you allow it. And for such a communication, we allow it, of course. Then – if you have a peaceful and loving state of mind – that will bring confidence to the soul of the dead, the ghost. And it makes it more likely, that a good conversation will take place. Be open for what the ghost tells you, try to understand, what he wants to tell and how he feels about the situation, you are talking about. The more understanding you can allow yourself, the more confidence this will bring to the ghost. And that is then a good condition to solve any problem for the ghost, that might be depressing him. What comes next is simply your talk with the ghost. You communicate, ask for information, give answers back if you think they help and try to solve the problem. That is pretty much it. It is amazingly easy, once you understand how that is done. It is no witchcraft", Bridget said with a smile on her face. "And after your talk, the next step is to create a pillar or ball or tunnel of light and ask the spiritual world for assistance to guide the ghost to the other side. If the ghost resists, let it. We do never force any ghost into anything. This is important, Aiden. We always keep a peaceful and loving state of mind and we fully respect if the ghost does not accept our attempts for a solution. Should you ever come into a situation, that you cannot resolve with a peaceful and loving mind, please come to me for help. Do not ever try to force something. It is so very important to have a basis of trust, that is your only chance to talk and communicate with a ghost and only if you have the trust of it, you can come to an agreement. Without trust, with anything other than peace and love, you will only get resistance and you will fight with an invisible opponent. You really do not want that, believe me."

Next day, when Aiden met with Bridget to continue his education, he asked her: "Bridget, as we have spoken yesterday about talking with the ghosts or souls of dead people, and since I have not heard anything about what happened to my father Owen, would you think it might be possible, that we contact him? It should work in case he is really dead, what do you think?"

"Yes, that is an interesting thought from you, Aiden. Let us try", Bridget agreed. Then she guided Aiden into a meditation to calm his mind and to open himself for the communication with the soul of his father Owen. Before they tried to establish this communication, Bridget reminded Aiden to imagine a ball of violet light around his physical body, which should protect Aiden from any kind of bad influences during the session. Then Bridget tried to contact Owen's soul: "Owen, father of Aiden from Galway, husband of Teagan, please come to us and talk with us. Owen, please, join us, that we can ask you some questions." Then Bridget said to Aiden: "Now, Aiden, to support our session, please visualize how your father Owen appears before your eyes. Please imagine, that the soul of your father Owen comes to join us and to talk with us." After a short pause, she continued: "What do you see, Aiden? Can you see your father?"

"No, I do not see my father, there is nothing", Aiden replied. "Why is that so?"

"I do not see him either, Aiden. Maybe your father is not dead, or he simply cannot come or does not want to talk with us. We cannot force it. We must accept it. Let us try something else, as we are already here", Bridget proposed, and she continued talking: "Father of Owen, grandfather of Aiden from Galway, please, come to us and talk with us. Father of Owen, we would like to ask you some questions, please."

Aiden was not sure, if his impression was real or only a fantasy, as he saw the soul of his grandfather appear in his imagination. He was wearing a linen shirt, leather pants, and boots. Aiden recognized his grandfather immediately, although he had not seen him in years since he had passed away.

"Can we ask you, please: Have you seen your son Owen coming to your world, is he with you in the hereafter?", Bridget wanted to know.

"As far as I can tell, Owen is not here. It was strange as I have seen him appear and disappear a couple of times, but he did not stay here, as far as I can tell. My impression was, that something pushed him into the hereafter and then he was pulled back again. I have never seen something like it before. But currently, Owen is not here", Aiden's grandfather said.

"Thank you very much, sir, for your talking with us. Do you have a message for your grandson Aiden too, please?", Bridget wanted to know.

"Yes, sure. Aiden, I am glad to see, that you are proceeding on your path to learn about spiritual practices and magic, and I am proud of you, that you show endurance in it. Let me say one thing, Aiden: Whatever happened to your father, please know, that everything is alright. There is no reason to worry as only good things can happen to Owen. Wherever he might be now, if he is alive or dead, I am sure, that this is, what the divine plan has foreseen for him and Owen makes the best out of it, as always. You see, Aiden, even when we are facing challenging situations, there is a high potential and possibility for us to learn and to grow ourselves. Even if we do not consider things to be good, they carry also good with them, and if it is only the chance for us, to learn from it. Instead of looking at your obstacles, Aiden, always look for the chances to learn from everything, you observe. Continue your learning, that will help you to understand more and more by time."

"Thank you, grandpa!", said Aiden. "How is it, to be dead?"

Aiden's grandfather replied: "What you call dead is life to me. One day, you will know, what this is like. I do not want to take away from you the experience, which you will make in your process of dying, Aiden. Therefore, I will not tell you more about how it is. Just try, that you get the chance to die with a clear mind. Do not try to numb your mind with alcohol or other poisons. The process of dying can be such an interesting experience, although it might frighten you, that you should never want to miss the chance to fully understand how it feels, when it happens to you."

"That is spooky and weird, grandpa. I am still so young; I hope to live on for some decades. I will be happy, once we are together again, grandpa, but it can wait. I miss my father and I miss you, too. My problem for now is, that I do not know, what happened to my father. I know that you have died, grandpa. That gives me peace of mind. But for my father I have not found that peace yet. This is, why I had hoped, you could help me", Aiden explained.

"Everything will turn out as it is foreseen, Aiden. Everything has a sense and if you look for the sense in all things, you might have a chance to understand one day. And maybe – if you continue your education you might also find a way to reconnect with your father, Aiden. Today, you have talked to me, even though I am dead already. One day you might be able to talk with your father Owen, no matter if he is dead or alive. As long, as he is missing, be confident, that you have a chance to find him, Aiden. Keep looking, keep learning. I love you, my grandson", Aiden's grandfather said.

"I love you too, grandpa. Thank you very much for your talking with us! Goodbye!", Aiden replied, then he saw, how the soul of his grandfather disappeared again. Aiden and Bridget slowly opened their eyes after they had taken some deep breaths.

"Wow, thank you Bridget, for this wonderful experience. It is not as spooky to talk with the dead as I had thought", Aiden admitted. Bridget smiled and nodded.

1477 – Colombo

At Aiden's fifteenth birthday, Donal took him aside and said: "Aiden, there is important news, I would like to share with you. You have now come to an age and we have things ahead, that urge me, to tell you something very important. We got news that sailors from Lisbon are on their way into the northern seas to explore and find Atlantis. Cristoforo Colombo is the captain of the ship and we believe, he somehow got knowledge of some old documents, which your father Owen was studying too. That is the reason, I believe, Cristoforo will find his way to Galway in his search for gold and prosperity, as those documents are describing some secret facts about the Order of the Templars, which landed here, one hundred and seventy years ago in 1307."

"What is the Order of the Templars?", Aiden wanted to know from Donal.

"The Templars were knights. Their task was to protect the religious pilgrims in the holy land, where Christ was born. These knights had been stationed at the temple of Salomon, where story tells that they found secret documents and other things, that made them very rich. As then the pope and the king of France got envious on them, the Templars got chased and killed. Some of them could flee, and some of those came to Galway. My grandfather had connections to these knights, that arrived here, and he also was the founder of our school of Magicians, as he had learned some interesting things about magic from these knights. We do not know a lot about the Templars as they lived hidden and secretly, mainly. But my grandfather was given some access to some documents, where we now have copies and which we use for your education as well, Aiden. And there is a story about a treasure, the Templars took away from France, loaded it on the ships and fled with that. There are some speculations and hints that parts of this treasure might also be here in Galway. And some people speculate that parts of this treasure are incredibly old and even come from the mysterious island called Atlantis. And now we believe, this is the reason for Cristoforo to come here, as he is very interested in power and money, so he is chasing for gold and everything, that could mean wealth to him and those men, that finance his doing. As it was your father Owen, that had the most insight in these things related to the Order of the Templars, I believe it is best, if you continue your father's work. You are still very young, Aiden, but given the facts we are facing now, I believe, it is time for you to take some responsibility to help our community stay safe and protected from those people, who are only interested in wealth. Their greed is a great threat to us and to humanity overall. We will get in contact with Cristoforo, give him some pieces of information and we believe, he might agree to let you join his crew on the ship, so you are part of the team and can observe directly, how things develop. And you should then be able to take action, should danger evolve for our community from what Cristoforo might be able to find in the northern seas. It also is a chance for us, to learn more about Atlantis, should Cristoforo really be able to find something about it. It is important for you, Aiden, to know, that we are not friends of Cristoforo or the people financing his voyages of discovery. He is not very smart; he is greedy, and he is a supporter of slavery. He is not much, what I would call a person with a good humanity. So, you should be very careful when you are in his company, Aiden."

"That sounds like a huge task for me, sir", Aiden said and took a deep breath. "Can someone from here join me on that voyage to assist and help me, if necessary, please?", Aiden asked from Donal with some concerns, as he felt frightened to be on his own among these sailors, on a journey he would not be able to control.

"Of course, Aiden. I would not expose you on such a dangerous mission without proper assistance. I have already spoken to Bridget and she agreed to accompany you. Sailors do not like women on board of their ships, as they believe that this brings bad luck to them and the ship, so we have to persuade them as we will indicate, that Bridget has some knowledge about Atlantis already. So with your father's knowledge about the Templars and Bridget's knowledge about Atlantis, I hope that should help us build a connection to Cristoforo, and that he hopes to take advantage of your knowledge, when he allows you to join the crew on this exploration."

And Donal should be right about all this. As Cristoforo's ship arrived in the harbor of Galway, Donal, Aiden, Bridget and many more came to observe the things coming. And as Cristoforo Colombo asked nearly every person in Galway about the Templars and about hidden treasures, and as he told some fairy tales of sea monsters and adventures, it was easy for Donal to give him the impression, it would have been his words and stories, that caught the interest of Donal's students and initiated Aiden's wish to join the expedition to the northern seas. Donal invited Cristoforo to a personal talk, where he then sat down with him, offering beer and secret information about the Templars of Galway, well selected information of course, and also some disinformation. Donal considered Cristoforo a serious threat and a chance for some important insight, too. In their private meeting, Donal arranged with Cristoforo for Aiden and Bridget to join the crew, while he assured Cristoforo, that the Templars did not have anything of worth with them, as they arrived in 1307 in Galway. He made him believe, that these Templars got separated from the other ships, that managed to flee from France and that on this ship only weapons had been loaded, no treasure, no gold, nothing of interest. And at the same time, he used Cristoforo's greedy attitude, to catch his interest for the secrets of Atlantis, as he indicated, the Templars would have told stories around this mysterious ancient island

and that Bridget and Aiden would know everything someone in Galway could know about these things.

Finally, Cristoforo felt incredibly lucky to have these two young people joining his expedition, as he stumbled drunken to the inn, where he would sleep tonight.

For Aiden, the expedition was also a chance to disappear for some time from Galway, which was a welcome alternation from his constant attempt to hide from Callahan, who had not yet stopped to look for the boy, although the great fire of Galway was already a couple of years ago. Callahan still observed Aiden's mother Teagan as he suspected, Aiden might return one day to get in contact with her. So far, the mayor had not been able to catch the boy, but he would not forget about him.

As Teagan was notified by Donal, that Aiden would go on a journey into the northern seas in a few days, she came to the school to visit her son. And she brought something covered in cloth.

In the presence of Donal, she handed the roll to Aiden. "What is that, mommy?", Aiden wanted to know from Teagan.

"This is a map from your father, Aiden. It indicates the position of the isle of Atlantis. No one really knows exactly, where it is or has been, or if it still is out there. But your father collected lots of information and did also a lot of research and this is at least, what he thought, might be the outcome of the position, that he tried to find. Maybe this map can be of help to you. That is, why I brought it here, Aiden", Teagan explained.

"Thank you very much, mommy. I will hide it away from the sailors and from Cristoforo, only Bridget shall know we have the map", Aiden said.

Aiden had never before been on a ship and he was excited about this new experience he would make. He and Bridget came on board of the ship and Cristoforo commanded one of his sailors to show them, where they would sleep on the ship during the journey. Cristoforo did not really show great interest in the two new passengers and Aiden and Bridget felt somehow lost from the beginning of their presence on this ship. Most of the sailors also looked suspicious at Bridget, as they did not really want to have a woman on bord. Aiden and Bridget were no longer sure, if that really was a good idea to join this crew. They decided to keep their distance as good as possible and Bridget explained to Aiden, how he could create a magical protection for himself, that would help to shield any bad thoughts of the sailors against them, during the voyage. Aiden was thankful for that, although he did not know, if that would really work.

It was only a short voyage on the sea when land came into sight. As Aiden and Bridget had asked a couple of times about the course and position of the ship, they had a good guess, where they might be, when the island was discovered on the horizon. Bridget knew from the drawings on the map, that cliffs and rocks would be under the water once they would approach the island from the current direction. As Cristoforo did not pay any attention to Bridget, she decided to go directly to the helmsman of the ship, to tell him about her concerns. He said, he would follow the commands of his captain only, and would not listen to a woman. Everything would be under control and she should not talk with him again. Bridget was worried, but what could she do? She decided to consult with Aiden about the potential danger ahead of the ship. As they still discussed the possibilities they would have, to create a wind, to drive the ship off course or to create a strong flow in the sea to drift the ship away from the hidden rocks, a strong jolt shook the ship, accompanied by a loud crash as the hull hit a rock. Bridget and Aiden were torn from their feet and fell in the belly of the ship. Both knew, what had happened as the helmsman came down to them and yelled: "It was the witch! She told me she would sink the ship at the cliffs if I would not change our course!"

Aiden looked to Bridget and both were caught by fear. What a primitive behavior of the helmsman and what a danger to their lives. As the water flooded the ship, the hull tipped over and the helmsman fell and hit his head hard. At least he was silent now. Aiden grabbed Bridget's hand and they ran upwards the wet stairs to the surface of the sinking ship. From there, it was a short escape into the water before the alerted sailors could lay hands on them.

Bridget and Aiden both knew how to swim, that would help them to survive. Nonetheless was it quite a distance to the island, so they had to struggle with the cold water and to take all their strength together to reach the shore. The sailors on the sinking ship tried to stop the water from flooding the ship's belly and had their hands full to deal with the damage. No one tried to follow or chase Bridget or Aiden. That was their luck so far. What a miserable end of this journey!

Finally, Aiden and Bridget reached the island. They were freezing, wet to the bone and Aiden noticed, that the map of his father, he carried in his clothes, was destroyed beyond recognition. "What now?", he asked Bridget.

"Let us leave the shore, and let us try to find a dry place, maybe a cave or a house, where we can sit at the fire to warm up", Bridget proposed, "but let us get out of sight of the sailors. These animals have no good intentions towards us! Believe me."

A few minutes later they found a little cave and some wood, which they collected to make a fire. In the cave, they looked at each other, and Aiden knew, what he had to do. He concentrated his thoughts, and although he was still breathing heavily because of the exhausting swim and run, he succeeded to clear his thoughts and concentrate. Flames started to consume the wood. Aiden felt the burning heat in his hand, and he knew, he was hurt once again by the flames. At least they had fire and a chance to dry their clothes and warm up.

As Bridget took off her wet clothes, Aiden was really tempted to stare at her wet skin. How beautiful she was. One short look from her eyes towards him, and his head flushed red. Aiden quickly turned his head away and stammered: "Sorry, sorry."

Bridget had a smile on her face. "Aiden, that's normal", she said. "You are attracted, what is wrong with that? I know about my effect on men, it is okay. Take off your clothes or you will catch a cold."

Aiden still felt ashamed, that he was not able to control his looks, but he also felt relieved that Bridget was not angry towards him. Instead, she showed understanding. Wow, what an amazing young woman she was.

After they had dried their clothes and felt warm and comfortable again, they discussed, how they would proceed. "The most important thing would be, that we avoid meeting these sailors again", Bridget said, "as they might still blame me for the accident of the ship. Besides that, it would be interesting, if we can find out anything about this island, if it has a relation to Atlantis or not, or if someone here knows anything about Atlantis."

"Yes, that seems to be a good idea", Aiden admitted, as he recognized, that he was still attracted by the presence of Bridget and he felt his blood pulsating between his legs.

"Cool down, Aiden", was the only comment from Bridget, as she knew what was going on with Aiden right now. It was the first time for this young boy to be in such an intimate situation with a young woman. She was fully aware, how confused Aiden was because of that.

As they left the cave to look around, Bridget proposed: "I could climb this hill here and take a look into the country, to see, where we are and where we should go from here." As she saw Aiden's surprise, she said: "We could both go up the hill, but what sense would it make? I must come down again anyway, so you can stay and rest until I will be back. It should not take me too long. You can observe the shore and warn me, should any sailors come near us, okay?"

"Ah, yes. That sounds good to me. At least I have a task that helps us too", Aiden agreed.

Bridget started to climb the hill while Aiden observed the shore. There was no sign of any sailor so far. Bridget climbed straight upwards and after a couple of minutes, she came to a cave, quite high on this hill. She decided to look inside. That was her doom. Something in the cave hit her hard and she was pushed backwards. There was no chance for her to stop her fall. With an immense power she fell down the rocks, Aiden saw how she hit the ground several times and he thought his heart would stop beating. As Bridget came down the hill quickly, so came stones with her and Aiden had to cover his head and try to protect from these deadly blows of the stones.

Then everything was silent again. No sound, no wind, not even the sound of a bird. It was so silent, Aiden felt, how fear crawled up his back into his neck. Shaking all over, he tried to find Bridget and he saw her laying between some rocks, not far from him. Blood was all over her face and she had her eyes closed. Did she breathe? Aiden could not see any move from her chest. As he came nearer, he felt more and more frightened. Should Bridget be dead?

No, she did not breath. She did not breath and was covered with blood. She had her head severely injured during her fall and there was no sign of life anymore. Aiden was about to panic. He felt so miserable as he looked at Bridget and then, he was overwhelmed by his feelings. No, he would not allow her to die.

No, he had to try to do something to safe her. Tears ran down his cheeks, he was still trembling over and over. Then, he carefully took Bridget's head into his hands. He closed his eyes and concentrated. "Bridget, please, listen to me!", he thought. "Bridget, please, stay with me, don't go into the light, please stay with me!" Then he visualized, as he had learned it from Cassidy, how the bones of Bridget's head where transposed where they belonged. He visualized, how the bleeding stopped, and the veins recovered from their wounds. Then, as he visualized, that all her bones were placed where they belonged, he imagined that a blue fluid would cover all the injuries on her head. This blue fluid would heal her wounds. He also visualized a string of white light, coming from heaven, flowing into the top of her head, a second string came from the earth and flowed into her feet. With this vitalizing energy, her recovery would be best supported by the healing light. Then he waited. Not long. He remembered, what he had learned from Bridget about communication with souls, entities and so on. He would not allow his thoughts to imagine Bridget to be dead or a ghost. In his imagination, Bridget's astral body simply was beside her physical body. He visualized Bridget's spiritual body and then asked her, to please come back, rejoin her physical body again. Aiden was not sure, if his visualization would have any effect, but as he opened his eyes for a short moment, he thought he had seen Bridget's body to slightly take a single, short breath.

Aiden held both his hands over Bridget's chest. He visualized a ray of green energy flowing from his hands directly to Bridget's heart. This would help her heart to start and continue beating. A second ray, a blue one, came out of his hands to support Bridget's lungs to help them breath, slowly, constantly, bringing fresh air into all the organs of the body. As he had the impression, that Bridget's condition was stable enough, he once again opened his eyes – and yes – yes – she was breathing!

Aiden covered his head with both of his hands and took a deep breath. He trembled still, and it was the first time, that he realized, that all his education on the school, even those topics, he never had much interest in, were so very helpful now. It was the first time, that Aiden really experienced, what power this knowledge had brought along. He knew that it was not his merit, that Bridget lived, it was solely Bridget's soul, that accepted to return and let her body heal. Aiden was only the link between the healing light and the accepting soul. Nothing more. But he was extremely thankful for having been given the chance to help with that. And he promised to himself, that he would continue his education, whatever it might take.

As Bridget continued to breath constantly and seemed to be in a stable condition, Aiden went to collect some leaves and plants, to build a soft underlay for Bridget's head. He then covered her body with his own jacket to keep her warm. Then he waited. He would not dare to move her back to the cave. He simply waited.

After about two hours, Bridget opened her eyes. Aiden was very happy about that. "Get Donal", she whispered silently. It took Aiden a while to understand. Then, he knew, what to do.

Aiden once again closed his eyes and concentrated his mind. "Donal", he thought, "we need your help! Donal! Please, hear me – we need your help!" Aiden visualized how he caught Donal's attention and that Donal recognized, what had happened. Then, Aiden lost his consciousness.

When Aiden woke up again, he was back at the school, and Donal was in the room. He also saw Bridget, and Cassidy took care of her.

"How did you do that?", Aiden asked Donal.

"Teleportation", Donal said. "Thank you for giving me the heads-up, Aiden. And good work! Well done, Aiden. I could not be prouder of you." Then Donal took Aiden in his arms and gave him a hug.

"Welcome", Aiden said with tears in his eyes. "Thank you all for the education. I really needed it. Thank you." Aiden felt that he was still trembling. Then he realized that his wounded hand was wrapped with a bandage.

Now he had a clear impression, what this was all about. He realized the real worth of all this knowledge, of all the positive and helpful things a magician could do with a solid education and training of skills. Somehow, Aiden was not the same as before. This accident had changed everything for him. He felt more alive than ever and he felt grown up.

After a couple of days, when Bridget had recovered quite well, and Aiden could talk with her, he asked her: "Bridget, what happened at the hill? Why did you fall down?"

"There was a dragon in the cave. He hit me with his tail. That hit pushed me back so fast and so hard, I could not do anything to prevent the falling", Bridget explained.

"A dragon; are you sure?", Aiden asked incredulous. "I thought, dragons where not real or at least only spiritual beings."

"Yes, I have never seen a dragon before, Aiden. As some ghosts can push people, I would say, this dragon, as physical or spiritual being, had the power to push me hard. Howsoever he did that, he must be a master in it", Bridget said. "I guess, he is guarding the entry of the cave. Whatever may be inside of it. He protects it and does not even ask, who is coming inside. Maybe, we will never know."

"Maybe Donal could take a look inside the cave, from here, from the distance?", Aiden proposed.

"I tried", Donal said, as he had listened in the back of the room. "I could not. Whatever there is, it is protected by a magic wall. No chance to look inside."

Next day, as Aiden could not forget about the dragon in the cave, he tried to get in contact with it by himself. So, he sat down for a meditation in his room and imagined, how he was on the island again, and how he climbed the mountain to get to the entrance of the cave. As he visualized how he came nearer, he proceeded with more care to prevent getting surprised by the dragon. He moved very slowly as he was near the entrance and he succeeded to get close enough, so he could carefully look inside. Aiden moved his head forward, slowly, very slowly, as he suddenly looked directly into the eyes of the dragon. The dragon saw Aiden and opened his mouth. Aiden was sure, that he would now be hit by a blast of fire coming out of the dragon's mouth. But he was not. The dragon was still calm and inspected Aiden's face with attentive eyes.

Now Aiden slowly showed his empty hands to the dragon and stood up, very slowly. He did not want to surprise the dragon with a spontaneous move or cause any kind of defense response as he still knew, what had happened to Bridget, when she was approaching the cave.

"Aiden is my name and I am here to ask you, who you are", he said to the dragon.

Then suddenly Aiden got pushed back hard by the dragon and as he felt losing his feet's contact to the ground, Aiden was ejected of his meditation.

That was strange, Aiden thought. At least the dragon did not seem to be an evil monster, but it seemed enormously powerful to Aiden. Maybe, one day, he and Bridget would get another chance to visit the island and get in contact with the dragon, Aiden thought. And he also felt that time was not yet right for that. Something was still missing, and Aiden believed, once they would have found out, what that could be, they could have a chance for permission to learn more about this cave and the secrets inside.

Indian Insights

With Aiden's sixteenth birthday, a new step in his education should begin. Cassidy told him: "Aiden, we believe, you are now ready to learn more about the connections of people's lives. I do not want to tell you too much right now. I would rather prefer to make this a surprise for you. Can we begin?"

"Yes, sure, I would like to begin!", Aiden said, and he was curious. Now, that he had experienced, how valuable all his education was, he was exited to enter the next level of his development as a magician.

Cassidy guided Aiden in a meditation into a state of deep relaxation. Then she instructed him, to go backwards in time, first slowly, by days, by weeks, months, years, then to his birth, and continuing into the time before his birth, back in time, back in time, faster and faster. Aiden should stop at that point in time when he was born for the first time ever. Cassidy again brought calmness into the situation. Aiden should only feel his own presence in the belly of his first mother, before his birth. Relax, sense the warm darkness and the wetness that surrounded him. Then Cassidy made him do a little jump in time to pass the process of his birth itself and to let Aiden continue his impressions shortly after his first birth.

"What do you feel now? Can you see daylight or something else?", Cassidy asked.

"Yes, I am somewhere, in a room and I see someone, a woman, she is my mother. She is so beautiful, and she smiles at me. I feel safe and curious. I am happy to be born now. My mother holds me on her belly, and she touches my skin softly. It is so good, to be there", Aiden described.

"Now we go forward in time, go to the time, when you are seven years old and tell me, how you live and where you live", Cassidy asked from Aiden.

"My name is Navin. I live in a tiny house with my mother and my siblings, there is a sister and two brothers. We often play in the dusty street outside the house. It is dry there and mostly hot, it is in India, the country is called India. We are happy as a family, although we are very poor. My mother has no husband, she works for a rich man, he comes and brings clothes of his servants to be repaired by our mother. And he has asked my mother already, when I would join him on a tour to buy spices and goods at the border of India. My mother tells him that I am too young for that. Our family belongs to a lower caste, that is the reason why we are so poor. We do not have access to good jobs or to good education. We are considered to have bad karma from our previous lives and so we have to live on this low level in society", Aiden explained.

Cassidy continued to guide Aiden further in time: "Now let us go forward in time, to a point in time, that is important for you, where things happen, that matter most to you, please."

After a short span of silence, Aiden talked again: "I am now fourteen years old and I have already been on a tour with the rich man to buy spices and goods. I was on a wagon with him and helped him to load and unload the goods, so he had not to do this heavy work. He is an unfriendly man. I do not like him much. Now, this evening, it is cold outside, and it is raining heavily. It is an ugly day, quite unusual, as if heaven itself was angry. Mother is not home yet, and I am in my bed, waiting for her. I am frightened from the bad weather but would not admit that to my siblings. I notice, how the door of our house is opened, and I see mother coming in. She looks horrible. Her face is dirty and wet, her clothes are torn. What has happened? She is crying and slowly goes to her bed. She forgot to close the door and wind and rain are coming in. Then the woman from our neighborhood comes in and closes the door. She must have seen our mother's arrival. They talk. She asks our mother, what had happened. I pretend to be asleep and listen carefully. My mother tells the neighbor that the rich man had raped her. She ran away back home and fell several times on her way, she is hurt, everything hurts, then she starts coughing. I am horrified. Tomorrow I shall go on another tour with the rich man again. I am shocked."

Cassidy asked: "What happens next day? Are you going on tour with the rich man?"

"Yes, I have to go", Aiden continued to tell, "and before that, in the morning, I am asking my mother, how she is. She is still coughing and says that she is fine, she only has a light cold from the bad weather yesterday. I know, this is a lie, she is not fine. She is suffering and she is sad. I must go; the man is here. He makes some unfriendly coldhearted comments and says that I must drive the second wagon. We would go with two wagons this time. It is the first time I drive a wagon with a horse and the wagon looks old and not very stable. The break, it is a stick of wood, is loose. I am concerned, it will not work properly, when we drive with the wagons through the mountains. The rich man drives first, I follow him. He does not talk much during our tour. It is a long way to the border, and we need a couple of days to arrive there. Then he has his contacts there, where he gets his goods. I have to load both wagons this time, while the rich man is in the village to drink some beers. I always have to think about, what he did to my mother, and I am in sorrow about her state. On our way home with the wagons I make a plan. When the rich man sleeps as we have to make a break I go to his wagon and remove the cotter from one of his wagon's wheels. I know, we come to a place, where the road has lots of curves and we would go downwards the mountains, and I hope, his wagon would lose the wheel and the rapist would fall in the abyss. Then it happens. The wheel falls off, the wagon falls to one side and the man falls to the street. He is still alive and did not fall in the abyss. I feel panic. He will accuse me for this accident and will punish me. I am certain. Then I remember the wooden stick of my wagon's brake. I take it out of its bracket, and I hit the rich man on his head with it. Again, and again. I hit him as hard as I can. He loses consciousness. He lies on the street and makes no move. Now I loosen the horse of his wagon and let it run. I place the rich man into his wagon, he is so heavy this fat huge man. Then I push the wagon to the abyss, as hard as I can. I press the heavy wagon, it barely moves, then, after some time, it falls into the abyss with the rich man on it. It crashes several times hard into the mountain and falls all the way down. Nobody would survive such a fall. I sit down and watch for a while, then I notice, it would have been easier to just throw the man over the border of the street into the abyss and not both, the man and the wagon, at the same time. But it was done now. The man has got, what he deserved. Now I climb on my wagon and continue my tour home. There I first run to our house to see, how our mother is doing. She has pneumonia and a severe fever, her head is wet from her sweat, she is shivering all over. I tell her, that the rich man is dead. She can barely hear me, I believe. I tell her I have killed him. I stay with our mother all the time until she is so weak, that she finally dies from her bad condition."

"Thank you for your telling, now it is time to return to our present time. Calm down, breath slowly and constantly and then we travel forward in time", Cassidy said. She affirmed to Aiden, that he would remember everything he experienced in this meditation, they had performed a couple of moments ago. Then she guided Aiden back into the present time, back to the room in the school. She also affirmed to Aiden, while he was still in his meditative condition, that he would remember more and more about his first live in India by time. Memories would come back, as he could deal with them, slowly, constantly, ongoing. That was an affirmation she made, to give Aiden a chance to learn more about the happenings from his own past life.

"How do you feel?", Cassidy asked Aiden, as he opened his eyes.

"I am somehow shocked, confused, but I am fine, thank you, Cassidy. It was so interesting to me. I would never have expected that I have such clear memories about a life I could not remember at all before. Do you really think that all this is true or was that just a dream or a fantasy right now?", Aiden wanted to know.

"This is something, you will find out by yourself, Aiden. Today, we have opened an important door together. Memories of this past life will come to you, normally in pieces, during the day, spontaneously and unexpected. You will learn to recognize them when they come. You will get used to them. I would like to ask you, Aiden, to work with those memories. Try to understand, what happened, why it happened, how you felt, when it happened, what your actions have been then and how you would assess your actions. Most people have no memory of their past lives and it is better so. As a magician and as someone with an open mind, you will be able to deal with these memories. I strongly believe so. And you are not alone with them, you have our community. Come to me, if you want to talk about anything, that you will remember, which would be hard for you to accept, maybe. Or talk to Bridget or Ide. They also have a lot of experience with those things and will be able to assist you, too. Okay?", Cassidy said.

"Yes, I will certainly do that, Cassidy. Thank you very much for this extremely interesting session today", Aiden said thankfully.

In the coming days, Aiden had more memories about his life in India. He knew, as he got pictures and impressions, that someone in India was present, when he told his mother, that he had killed the rich man. This old woman heard, what he said and told it to others from the village. He then was hunted and had to flee. There have been a lot of things happening after all that and the most important thing, Aiden realized, was, that he went from India to Afghanistan and met a wonderful young woman there. He saw her face, she had the prettiest face he had ever seen, and she was kind and intelligent. Since the moment, he saw her face for the first time, he could not forget her anymore – until he died in India and the memory remained covered deeply inside his soul.

Aiden knew, he had a long and happy life with this woman in Afghanistan, they have lived in prosperity in a village, where people were friendly and helped each other. They had no castes there and everybody had the same rights. What a difference, what a pleasure to live there.

Another day, as Aiden met Donal in the school, he asked him: "Donal, can you tell me – if it is our first life ever, can it be, that we already have a bad karma?"

"What a question, Aiden? If it is your first life and you never had a life before, how would you be able to carry any karma from past lives with you? Think about it. I believe, it is not possible. When a young soul comes to earth it is clean as pure water. It has no experience yet, no sins done so far. There will be a lot of joy and experimentation in the first life and a lot of mistakes, too. Karma, in the first life? No, I do not believe so. But – as I have told you before – please draw your own conclusion. That is important! Does that help you, Aiden?"

"Yes, it does, Donal. Thank you very much", Aiden said. And he knew now, that in his opinion, the castes in India are no good. A new life should always be a fresh start, for anybody and any soul. Karma will reward our actions, people have no need to reward anyone on top of that, he concluded for himself.

Callahan's Wrath

When Aiden was seventeen years old, things changed dramatically. He lived now in the community of the Galway magicians since a couple of years already. He was well integrated and among good friends, he thought. But evil was on its way.

A ship came into the haven of Galway this year, and on board was a sailor from the former crew of Cristoforo Colombo. As things turned out, this sailor saw Bridget on the market square and recognized her as the witch, who sank the ship, two years ago. As he went to catch her, she saw him and ran away. She was lucky and could hide herself from the sailor, but he went directly to Callahan, the mayor of Galway. He reported that he saw a witch, Bridget was her name as he remembered, and demanded, the people of Galway should turn her over, together with the boy, Aiden.

Now the sailor had Callahan's full attention. Did he say Aiden? Yes. He did. That was the lousy boy's name, who he was looking for so long. Should Aiden still be in Galway? If he was seen together with a witch, two years ago, it might be possible, that the lousy boy was hiding in the school of the Galway magicians. Callahan decided to act. And he would not do it obviously, but more hidden and in secret. He promised the sailor, that he would take care of the witch and the boy and deliver them, as soon as they were found. Then he sent out someone with a letter to Glen-Bill, a robber and thief, who lived outside the town, as he was not very welcome due to all his bad deeds, that he was known for.

Glen-Bill was an unkempt, ugly, yellow-toothed man who thought he was omniscient and yet had a limited mind. He stole not only money from the people he met, but also their time, with his long monologues and his useless ramblings. Then, when no one expected it, he accused the people and forced the money out of their pocket to make amends. He was a common deceiver of the worst kind and never paid his guilt to others.

For Callahan, he was the right partner for the lousy job that he now wanted to see done.

As Glen-Bill was too dumb to read, he asked one of his companions, to read the mayor's letter to him, which he had received from the mayor's servant, after he had involved the servant in a long and annoying speech, where he bragged with his knowledge about things, that nobody was interested in. The servant left the place with a long sigh, finally.

As Glen-Bill heard from his fellow, the mayor wanted him to catch Bridget from the school of magicians in Galway and this boy, Aiden, who had disappeared after the huge fire in Galway. This boy would most likely also be hidden in the school's area, the mayor suspected. At the end of the letter, the mayor wrote, he would reward Glen-Bill with a decent amount of money as soon as the job would be done.

Glen-Bill smiled with his yellow teeth and coughed because of the dirty herbs he smoked all day.

Then he called a few of his fellows and they started their walk towards the school. As they could not enter the school's area without permission, they waited, hidden behind bushes. Had Bridget already returned to the school or was she still out? If necessary, Glen-Bill and his crew would enter the school's area by night to abduct the witch and search for the boy.

Better would it have been to catch her right away before she could return behind the walls of the school's area. Then, with a little luck, others would come to search for her, and he would simply pick the boy out of them. Aiden was known in Galway, although he had not been seen for quite some time. Glen-Bill would recognize him, he was sure about that.

Then the scamps noticed someone coming from the town towards the school. It was a young woman. Yes, that was

Bridget. As she came closer, Glen-Bill jumped out of the bushes, right in front of her. "Hello sweety!", Glen-Bill said, and Bridget could see his dirty yellow teeth.

"Don't sweety me!", Bridget said, and her face got angry. "Let me pass, I do not have time to spend with you. Step aside", she demanded.

But Glen-Bill did not step aside. He still stood in front of her, grinned and spit on the floor. Then Bridget was grabbed from behind and one of the bastards put a sac over her head. Then her hands got tied, the sac got tied around her hips, then she was forced to the ground and her feet got tied too. Bridget wanted to shout for help, but as she made the first attempt, a fist landed on the sac and hit her mouth. Blood came through the sac as she was dragged away by Glen-Bill and a fellow of him.

The other thieves waited in the bushes for the boy, they hoped to grab too.

Glen-Bill and his fellow returned to Glen-Bill's house, where they locked Bridget away in a small hutch near the house. "When we come back with the boy, we will have some real fun with you, sweety, before we deliver you to the mayor!", Glen-Bill laughed dirty. What an asshole! Then Glen-Bill and his fellow left Bridget in the hutch and returned to the school to help catch Aiden.

Bridget recovered from her pain. She would not let that be good, she decided. She moved herself into a sitting position and concentrated. The rope around her hips, that held the sac, got loose, as if it was opened by the hands of a ghost. The rope fell off, and the sac flew from Bridget's head in a wide bow. Now she could see again. The hutch had a window, and she could see a pigpen outside, close to the house of Glen-Bill. How this dirty, ugly bastard would regret, what he did to her, she promised herself!

Bridget concentrated again and dark clouds gathered in the sky. First tiny raindrops fell, then larger ones, and then it was pouring with rain. The pigs' excrement was washed out of the pigpen directly into the front door of Glen-Bill's ugly hut.

Oh, yes, how he would regret it! Then Bridget thought of Glen-Bill's next action, as he had indicated to catch Aiden, too. She concentrated again and visualized a long, hot needle and how this needle got stuck into Glen-Bill's back. And another huge hot needle was thrust into his leg with momentum. And another one into his neck. And one in his head. Then Bridget imagined, how the needles got deeply red, they glowed and started to smoke.

Glen-Bill had just returned to his group of thieves near the walls of the school, as he saw huge clouds raining down heavily in the area, where he lived. Should the witch be responsible for that? Then, suddenly and without warning, he felt a sharp pain in his back. "Ahh!", Glen-Bill shouted and tried to reach the hurting point in his back. Then he felt the pain in his leg and that made him fall. His dirty face landed in a muddy puddle. And then he felt his neck and his head aching. And as he thought, that was all, the pain grew immensely, it burnt him so heavily, that he had to cry out, as loud as he could. "Ahh!!!" His cry was heard all over the countryside, even in the school.

Cassidy was the first to arrive at the school wall's door and she opened a small window in it to look outside. She recognized Glen-Bill, this ugly thief, and his dirty fellows and then she called for Donal.

Donal opened the door and stepped outside, directly towards this group of miserable pricks. "What is it?", he asked calmly.

"Oh, nothing, sir", said one of these cowards. "Glen-Bill fell, and I think he hurt his leg a little bit. Nothing severe, I would say", lied the dirty short man.

"Yeah, he should be more careful, where he steps his feet, I would say. This can be a rough way, so close to our school for people that cannot read, I suppose", Donal insulted the group. He was definitely not afraid of them and he knew exactly, what they had done. He also saw Bridget coming closer on the way to the school and went calmly towards her. The thieves looked at each other and were confused. What should they do now?

"Hello Bridget", Donal said to her, "is everything alright with you?"

"Yes, sure, I am fine, Donal, thank you", Bridget replied as a thick flash went down from the sky in the distance with a huge thunder and hit the hutch near Glen-Bill's house. This sat the hutch on fire and it slowly burnt down, while Donal and Bridget leisurely walked back to the school's area, arm in arm.

Callahan jumped off his chair as he got the notice from the dirty little thief about what had happened when Bridget was abducted. He grabbed his chest and gasped and it made him feel dizzy.

Now he would take it in in his own hands. He was outrageous of anger and walked directly to Teagan's house. There he shouted and yelled like an idiot and threatened Teagan, that he knew, that Aiden was hiding in the school with the Galway magicians, and that he would tear down all houses until Aiden was found.

This fat, dumb mayor made an incredible scene in front of Teagan and she decided to leave as soon as this idiot would be gone. She listened calmly to Callahan's words, then after a while, she decided to stop his speech.

"Oh, my goodness, the water burns on the stove!", she said suddenly and closed the door before Callahan could even finish his last sentence.

Teagan waited in the house until Callahan left, cursing and gesturing wildly.
Then Teagan decided to pack some things together and leave the house. She went to the school to talk to Donal and wanted to propose, that she and Aiden would leave Galway until things would have changed for the better, hopefully.

Bridget proposed, she would accompany Teagan and Aiden on their journey, as it was also better for her to disappear, until the sailor would be back at sea with the ship.

"By the way", Donal said, with a smile on his face. "You remember, the ship of Colombo, that sank at the island, with you and Aiden on board?", he asked Bridget.
"Yes, sure", Bridget replied.
"It will not be Cristoforo's last ship to sink. As far as I have seen, he will sink nine ships in his career as a captain, at least. So – he will have a lot of witches to hunt for his bad luck, I suppose", said Donal.
"Nine ships! Wow. Bad luck or bad karma, that's the question", Bridget said.
"Guess it's karma. It should not be his first life as a slave trader. His soul was not pure like water or innocent, I would say. To me, he seemed more like an old soul, filled with grudge, grim and greed", Aiden added.
"Whatever made him so", said Donal.

From Fairies and Elves

Aiden and his mother Teagan had found shelter at an aunt. Since several month's had passed by already, Bridget had been able to return to the school in Galway in the meantime and Aiden was now eighteen years old.

There was a knock on the door. Aiden jumped up from his chair and went to the door to open it. He saw Ide standing in front of him and he spontaneously gave her a hug. "Ide, what a surprise!", Aiden said and smiled, then he looked at her. "What a pleasure to see you here, please, come in! Do you want a cup of tea or something to eat?", asked Aiden.

"Tea would be fine", said Ide. "Bridget could describe me the way to your place over here, so we, Donal and myself, thought it would be a good idea, to continue with your education right here. What do you think? Would you like to meet some fairies and elves, Aiden?"

"Fairies and elves? Wow, yes, that sounds wonderful. I would like to meet them, yes, sure", Aiden said, full of joy to have Ide here in the house with him.

"Okay then. I can stay some time, if that is okay for your aunt and your mam, and we can go out in the nature to visit the fairies and elves in the coming days or weeks. Great", Ide said.

Both sat a while at the table and Ide had to tell Aiden about the news from Galway and the school. He was so interested in anyone's lives, so they talked really a long time, until Teagan and aunt Kevina returned home. They also welcomed Ide and Kevina offered her to stay as long as she would like. It was normal here in Ireland, that all members in a house would participate in all the work that had to be done to keep life going on, so it would not be a load to have two diligent hands more in the house.

In the coming days, Ide and Aiden went out into the fields of this part of Ireland, that was known for its forests and cliffs. One of their first walks was into the forest. Ide showed Aiden a couple of plants and explained to him, that there are elves who are taking care of the plants, their growing, the fruits and everything. She told Aiden to sit down calmly, as they were by some very pretty flowers. Ide asked Aiden to close his eyes and get calm and quiet. Then Ide tried to contact some elves. Somehow it seemed to Aiden, that these elves might already know Ide from some previous visits, but he might also be wrong with that. He had the impression, that there would be some elves here, right now. So, he carefully and slowly opened his eyes. And – yes – he saw some very fine and delicate beings. How cute they were. Tiny little elves, woven from light and energy it seemed.

Then Ide talked to them and she did it with her normal voice, so that Aiden could also hear, what she said. She spoke very friendly to the elves, asked about their well-being and if there was anything unusual for them at these times. Then she asked them about these flowers, anything one could imagine, how old they were, when they bloom and if there is also a healing capability within these flowers. It was very interesting for Aiden to watch Ide communicate with these elves. There was no loud or rough tone in her voice, she was talking so full of loving feelings, Aiden thought for a moment, Ide herself could be an elf. Then Ide thanked the elves for the good talking with them and said goodbye to them, expressing once again best wishes to them, from herself and from Aiden.

The next day, Ide and Aiden went deeper into the forest until they came to a place with a small pond. "Those places in the woods with water, like this pond, are ideal for meeting fairies", Ide explained to Aiden. "Sit down, we will see, if we can get in contact with a fairy", she proposed.

Aiden sat down, got calm and watched the silent water and the plants, which slightly moved the leaves in the gentle wind.

What was that? A fairy! Wow, indeed, Ide had found the place of a fairy! Aiden was really impressed. Then Ide started talking with the fairy. It was a longer talk and Aiden got the impression, that the fairy was extremely interested in all the stories Ide told her. At one point, as they talked about all kinds of topics, even about the school of the Galway magicians, the fairy said: "Do you know, that there is a cave near Galway, where the Templars have left a hidden treasure?"

Aiden could not believe his ears! It was quite a distance to Galway and surely another distance to this cave, the fairy mentioned. How could she know about that?

"Oh, we know, that Templars have landed in Galway, quite some time ago and we also know, that they carried knowledge with them in books and so. But I did not know that there is a treasure, hidden in a cave", Ide said frankly and open minded.

"Yes, it is", the fairy continued. "The dwarfs told us that. They are protecting the treasure, so it might not fall in false hands. You surely know, as the elves are taking care of plants, the dwarfs are taking care of the treasures of the earth, mainly precious minerals, but also other treasures. To me, you seem to be a trustworthy person, so I believe it is okay to let you know about this treasure. I guess." The fairy seemed to be a little bit shy, as she said that, or insecure, if she had just revealed a secret.

"Oh, thank you so much", Ide continued. "You are too kind. It might be indeed helpful to visit these dwarfs and ask them about the Templar's treasure. But we also must be very careful, when we do that, as not all humans are good minded. We also have some evil people in Galway. But I can promise you, that we will be really careful to bring no danger or harm to the dwarfs or to the treasure, they are protecting."

"There are no doubts about that, young lady", the fairy kindly said.

Aiden was impressed and overwhelmed. Ide really had the right tone and sensibility to establish trust between herself and the fairy. What a wonderful young woman she was, indeed.

"Ah, there is one more thing, I should also tell you about this", the fairy started talking again. "You are Aiden, right? The son of Owen, yes?"

"Yes, that is me. I am Aiden, son of Owen, yes", Aiden said, surprised, that the fairy now talked directly with him. He had not expected that from such a fine entity.

"Aiden, you should know, in order to get access to the treasure of the dwarfs, you must be willing to die. If you are not, you will fail", the fairy warned.

Aiden was surprised and somehow disturbed. "Why is that so?", he asked from the fairy.

"It is the only way to find out about the purity of your heart and soul. Only if the dwarfs get the right to end your life instantly, they will allow you to proceed. And if you are not worthy, they might kill you. So, you better think carefully, if you really want to attempt to get access to that treasure, Aiden. Many have died before, I know that. You should know that too."

A shiver ran down Aiden's back. And he thought until now, that talking to a ghost would be creepy!

The next day, Ide took Aiden for a walk to the cliffs. As they arrived there, Ide spread her arms into the wind and said: "What a wonderful day, today. The fresh wind, the clean air. It is beautiful in the nature, isn't it?", she said.

Aiden saw Ide's clothes blowing in the wind. He had the impression he could look through the thin fabric and he clearly saw the contours of Ide's body. Wow, what an image.

Aiden felt the blood gathering between his legs, a feeling he knew from his experience with Bridget in the cave on the island.

Aiden noticed that his face got hot and he knew for certain, that it went deeply red right now. He was still such a shy young man. He hoped, Ide would not see his red skull, but she did.

"Aiden?", Ide asked, and Aiden felt caught. After a pause, he said: "Yes?"

"Would you like to see the death, Aiden? Would you like to know how that is, the last moment in your life, before the angel of death is coming to take you with him?", Ide asked.

Aiden felt insecure, what he should think about this question. Was Ide about to make a joke to him or did she want to threaten him?

Aiden was confused, maybe some seconds too long, and Ide continued: "You know, if you want to face the dwarfs and be ready to die, you should probably know, what you are going to do then!", she said.

She must be serious, Aiden thought. That was no joke and it was no threat. It was a serious question and he was asked if he would like to make a death experience. What a woman!

"Okay", Aiden heard himself saying. Now he felt not only his skull was hot and red, but heat went all over his body, up and down and he felt that his shirt went wet from that! Was that a new form of fear, he never had before?

"Great, okay", Ide said. "Then come here, stand here by the cliffs and step back a little bit", she asked from Aiden. He did as he was told and stood with his back to the cliffs, so he could see Ide, but not the deep abyss. "Okay, step back a little bit more, Aiden", Ide asked again. "Step back, go."

As Aiden was standing awfully close to the edge of the cliffs, suddenly and unexpected a stone breaks and he slips off. By fortune or luck, he can just hold on to the cliff edge with his hands. Then he sees the angel of death, startles and lets go of the rock.

Ide quickly grabs Aiden's arm and holds him. The angel of death disappears, and Ide pulls Aiden up.

Aiden sat now silently and shocked at the edge of the cliffs and then he crawled away from the edge, trembling all over.

"How was that?", Ide asked.

Aiden was still shocked as he replied: "That was insane. It came so quickly, and it frightened me totally!"

"You know, Aiden, the angel of death is not your enemy. He is there to help you, so that you do not have to die alone. He is, indeed, your best friend. As he will be there in your final hour, in your last moments of this life and he will not ever let you alone in that moment. You do not have to call for him, you do not have to ask him to come – he will be there. That is his task and his most important wish. To never let you die alone. You understand that, Aiden?", Ide asked with tears in her eyes. She was obviously moved as she talked so clearly about Aiden's dying. How Aiden loved this woman. He stared at her face. Longer than he should.

"You want to try it again?", Ide asked. Then she smiled. Could she read his mind? Was that her way to say: "Don't you even think about anything like coming closer to me!"

"No, no, no, no, no", Aiden said quickly, still frightened and confused. "Have you seen the angel of death too, before?", Aiden wanted to know from Ide.

"Yep. I have. Mine is different from yours. Mine is a woman. A pretty one", she said shortly. And after a while she continued: "And - do not fall in love with me, Aiden. Focus on your education. That is more important for you. Believe me that."

Then she stood up and made a sign to Aiden with her head to follow her home. She could read his mind; Aiden was sure about it. And he felt somewhat disappointed, that she was not in love with him, as far as he could tell.

Callahan's Legacy

In the past couple of months Aiden had learned a lot about plants and their healing capabilities and about poison in plants and other effects of them. It was an interesting time and he enjoyed every day and every hour, when Ide came by to visit him from time to time.

When she was not here with him, Aiden continued his working with the fire magic book from his father, that he had received from his mother a couple of years ago. To read the book was one thing, to practice with the book was another thing.

Besides that, Aiden wanted to find out more about his previous lives. As he had evolved his practice since his first sessions with Cassidy, where she helped him get insights in his first life in India, he was now able to go back in time by himself, to explore previous lives.

This was a great advantage as he could collect his impressions with his own speed and whenever he had an opportunity to do so.

Aiden was now nineteen years old and already a young magician with quite some knowledge and capabilities. He was still far from perfect, but he had made huge progress in the past years, in many ways, most importantly in his character. He was grown up and had a much better understanding of the universe, the energies that flow and hold everything together, the connections between human beings, spanning lives over centuries, the rules and rewards of karma, the spiritual entities and much more.

Today, Aiden wanted to explore one other life of his past, he had not yet investigated. He had got an image, a couple of days before, about a previous life, where he obviously seemed to have been a woman. That felt strange and unusual to him, so he wanted to know more about it. He took the chance, when his aunt and mom where out of the house and he was undisturbed, to sit down and to guide himself into a deep state of meditation.

He went back in time, more and more, further and further, until he arrived in the time of his life as a woman. Then he looked.

Aiden saw himself as a young woman, who was pushed out of her home town as she had born a baby from a man, who had persuaded her to sleep with him and then did not want to marry her, as she got pregnant. The town's community had no understanding for that, she was considered a whore and the people rejected any contact with her. She could no longer go to buy some bread or milk, as she was not welcome in the town's stores. Her sister, who had supported her during her pregnancy had left the town as she could no longer stand the shame, which her sister and her bastard child brought over her too.

So, the young woman with Aiden's soul, Penny was her name, decided to leave the town too. She had no idea, where to go to and spent quite some time in the woods with her baby, collecting berries and fruits, and whatever she could find. That was not a solution that would last. She knew that. So, she went on looking for a better place where she could stay with her child.

One day, she came into a small village, a not so clean one, but people seemed to be friendly. It was at the coast of this country and usually the streets were filled with strangers, sailors from foreign countries, that came here to trade with goods of different kinds. As she walked through the streets, she came by a whorehouse. It was obvious to her, as she saw the painting of a naked woman at the front of the house, nearby the entry door. Should she go inside? She was called a whore so often, that she began to believe to be one, finally. Yes, she would have the courage to go in. And so, she did.

Inside the whorehouse was a young woman behind a bar. Penny asked if she could stay and work here. She would do any work, whatever it would be. She only wanted to have a chance to feed and raise her child in an environment, where she was not pushed away because of the fact, that the child had no father. She was greeted and received with surprising friendliness by the woman behind the bar. She was told she could get a room with a small extra chamber for her little child and that she should take her time to arrive and rest from her voyage.

She and her son were given food and something to drink and Penny felt happy to have finally arrived in a place, where she could hopefully stay longer. After this friendly welcome and the dinner, she went to her room with her boy and took a long sleep.

Next day in the morning, when Penny woke up, she went downstairs to see, how she could arrange her further stay. The friendly woman asked her, if she knew, what a whorehouse is, and if Penny was willing to earn some money working as a prostitute. Anything was better than to starve on the street, Penny thought and decided, she would give it a try. She had not much to lose anyway. Her only concern was her young child. She would do anything to feed him and grow him up.

So, she made the deal with the friendly woman. She got an arrangement, that sailors that came into the house would be sent to her, as well as to the other women in this establishment.

As the first sailor came into her room, Penny felt insecure but tried to stay calm. The sailor was quite friendly to her and payed her well for her service. Penny felt dirty after that. She needed to wash her body intensely. The friendly woman from the bar downstairs came by and brought her fresh towels and soap. She told Penny, that she knew how she felt after her first time with a stranger. She said Penny would get used to it, by time. Penny hoped, she was right.

As days and weeks went by Penny really got somehow used to her new job. Nevertheless, sometimes it felt not right. There were sailors that were quite normal, others were very demanding or grabbed her so strongly that she got bruises on her arms and sometimes on her legs as well.

The feeling, that she had to wash her body intensely never got away. For some sailors she felt pity, for others she felt disgust.

Then came the day when the richest man in town came by. That was the pure horror for Penny. This fat huge man was very demanding and talked with Penny in a humiliating way. Penny felt nausea growing inside her and finally, as the fat man was gone, she had to vomit.

And that was not the last time she saw the fat, rich swine. His next visit was as unpleasant as the visit before and Penny trembled for about half an hour after he was finally gone.

On the third visit of this fat humiliating man the horror exceeded Penny's pain limit many times over as this fat swine brutally raped Penny and did not even pay her. Penny cried so loud, that the friendly woman from the ground floor came upstairs to look after her. She explained to Penny, that she could not really change the situation or help effectively as this rich swine had the power to close the whorehouse and throw them all out on the street.

Penny felt horrible and hopeless. In the evening, when all these women sat together as usual at the dinner table, a black-haired woman took Penny aside. She told her, that she had also been mistreated by the fat swine a couple of times, before Penny arrived in the whorehouse and that she had two knifes and would kill the swine next time, he would try to hurt her. Then she handed the knifes over to Penny as she knew that the swine would rather continue to visit Penny than to come to her again.

Penny took the knifes with shaking hands. She had lost all her nerves and if it had not been for her young boy, she would have used the knifes to cut her own throat with them to end her life. She thanked the black-haired woman and went to her room. The knifes looked like little sickles with their curved blades. Penny placed one knife at the left border of the bed and the other knife on the right border. Should the ugly fat swine ever hurt her again, Penny would use the knifes, she was determined.

And the day came sooner than she thought. The rich swine once again came to Penny and without greeting her he threw her on the bed and insulted her again with humiliating words. Then he took off his trousers and came over Penny. He penetrated her hard, and horrible pain filled Penny's abdomen. Tears shot in her eyes. With trembling hands Penny searched for the knifes and she found them. With one knife in each of her hands she reached out and with all her strength she rammed the curved blades into the sides of the fat swine's body. The man cried and Penny pulled out the blades quickly, crossed her hands before her face and cut the throat of the ugly swine from both sides. Blood spurted out and spilled all over the bed. The swine made his last twitch and then fell heavily on Penny's body. She had to struggle to throw him off and the fat body slammed onto the floor. It was done. Never ever again would this fat ugly asshole hurt any woman again.

With blood all over, Penny went to the bathroom, where she sank down and cried for a long time. No other woman came by. She was alone and she needed that.

As Aiden returned from his meditation, he was shocked. "I killed another man. I don't believe it", he said to himself. He needed his time to digest that, so he decided to go out for a walk. He wanted to have some fresh air and felt miserable and disturbed from all these impressions he got a couple of minutes ago.
"I was a prostitute and killed another man. What bad karma must I have. Now I understand, why most people have no memory about their previous lives. It is simply better so", Aiden said to himself.

Aiden went to bed early this evening, but he could not sleep. He had to think about this previous life again and again and he could not get these impressions out of his head, now, that they had been set free.
Finally, extremely late in the night, he did fell asleep.

Next morning Aiden woke up and felt horrible. But there was another thing. He suddenly knew it. This last meditation opened a new door, with power, with immense power. And it was a lot, Aiden had to take from that. He had felt prepared for the looks into his previous lives, but it was harder, than he had thought, to deal with these impressions, finally.
And now he knew. More than he wanted to know at first. He realized now that his mother in India was no other soul, than Teagan's, his mother from his present life. It was all so clear to him now. And the friendly woman behind the bar in the whorehouse and the dark-haired prostitute, who gave Penny the knifes, that were Bridget's and Ide's souls. Aiden was quite sure about that now. Finally, the rapist from India and the fat

swine from the whorehouse, these two disgusting monsters, that was Callahan's soul. He had killed him twice now and he felt, he could kill him again and it would not bother him at all.

Aiden spent the day quietly, thinking about all his impressions. He wanted to talk to someone about all this, but to whom? His mom and his aunt would not be the right persons for that, he believed. Ide and Bridget maybe? Yes, that would be a better choice. Maybe they also knew about their previous life in the whorehouse? But they were in Galway and he was not.

Aiden decided to go back to Galway, to talk to Ide and Bridget about his new insights and to face Callahan, finally, again.

Aiden wanted to be prepared, before he would return. He had noticed that his aunt had a leather glove for her left hand beside the fireplace. He asked her directly: "Aunt Kevina, may I ask you something?", Aiden started.

"Yes, sure, what is it?", Kevina wanted to know.

"I see, you have a glove at the fireplace for your left hand. Do you use it for the fire?", Aiden asked.

"Yes, it protects my hand from the heat of the flames, when I put wood in the fire", Kevina explained.

"And you do not use the glove for your right hand, then?", Aiden continued.

"No, I do not need it. I like it to have the right hand free and I only need one hand for the wood. So, I am fine with this one glove. Why do you ask, Aiden?", Kevina wanted to know.

"Well, if you don't mind – I could use a glove for my right hand, to be honest. I have a strange talent to always burn my right hand, when I play with fire, aunt Kevina, you know?", Aiden said carefully.

"Ah, okay, sure, you can have it. Wait – I'll get it for you", Kevina offered. Then she stood up, went to a drawer of her cabinet and grabbed the right glove, which she then handed over to Aiden.

"Thank you very much, aunt Kevina. That is a fine leather glove and I am certain, that it will serve me very well. Many thanks", Aiden said.

"You're welcome", replied Kevina.

In the coming days, Aiden used his fathers' book about fire magic to prepare the glove for his usage with the fireballs. He imprinted the glove with his concentrated mind to be better protected from the heat of the flames. With that, Aiden should be able to create more and larger fireballs without burning the skin of his hand again. Aiden did a lot of exercises with the imprinted glove to see if it worked. He imprinted, created fireballs, small ones, bigger ones, imprinted, created fireballs and so on – over and over. It took Aiden about two full weeks until he was content with the result. He could now create huge fireballs with his right hand and had good control over them without hurting his hand, as the imprinted magic glove worked fine. Aiden was very content, and he felt ready to return to Galway for the final showdown with Callahan.

But – there was another thing that had to be done before that. Aiden wanted to get a stick of wood, like the one, that was used for the break of the wagon he drove, when he killed the rapist in India. And he wanted to get two knifes with curved blades, the same as he had used to kill the fat swine in the whorehouse. Yes, he needed those items first, and then he would confront Callahan, finally.

The wooden stick was not hard to find, knifes with curved blades were a bigger challenge. For these Aiden went back in time, four weeks only, and he imagined a traveling dealer buying those knifes and bringing them to the store in the next town nearby. As Aiden came back from his visualization, he was quite confident, that the knifes would be there in the store, as he had imagined. He would give it a try.

Early next morning Aiden walked to the town and went directly to the store, where he assumed, that he would find the knifes. He entered the store and asked if they would sell knifes with curved blades. The dealer behind the bar smiled and said yes, he had got some nice knifes of this kind, just a couple of days ago from a traveling dealer that came by. Aiden smiled. It had worked. Aiden saw the two knifes and they looked exactly like those from Penny. He took them both gladly and payed for them accordingly.

Now Aiden felt prepared and strong. In the early afternoon he decided to tell his aunt and mom that he would go to visit the school of the Galway magicians. Teagan and Kevina were a little bit surprised, but why not? Perhaps time had changed after all these months and it finally would be good, if Teagan could also return home. If Aiden would find out about that possibility, it would be great. Teagan told Aiden to be careful and he promised to his mom he would be.

As Aiden arrived at the school of the Galway magicians, he knocked on the door and Donal opened it and gave Aiden a hug. Then he said: "Aiden, welcome back. It is good to see you. I was already expecting you to come. Would you like to join me for a cup of tea, please?" Donal invited Aiden with a gesture to follow him.
"Yes, sure. Good to see you too, Donal, and yes, I would like to have a cup of tea with you", Aiden replied.
Both took a walk to the central school building, where Ide and Bridget also were already waiting for Aiden, who ran towards them to give them also a hug.

"Ide, Bridget, what a joy to see you again!", Aiden said with a smile on his face, that was still dusty from his journey.

They sat together at the table and Donal began to speak: "Aiden, I would like to have a word with you. Please do not be upset, that I am talking so straight forward. It is – I am concerned about some things going on currently."

"I will not be upset, Donal. Please continue, what is it?", Aiden replied.

Donal took a deep breath before he said: "I know that you have continued your education, while you have been away from Galway. Bridget and Ide informed me about your good progress, and I am awfully glad about it, honestly. And then I saw that you also did some exercises to go back into your previous lives, to learn more about these too. And I am totally fine with that. It is only, that it might be good for you, to not act upon your latest findings too quickly. Some of our lost memories, which we get back through our insights into previous lives may be disturbing and may cause us some trouble, I would say – out of my own experience. I know, that you have seen", and Donal took a deep breath, before he continued his talking, "Callahan in your previous lives and that you have killed him, or his previous incarnations, twice already."

Aiden looked extremely interested into Donal's eyes. He considered Donal as his mentor and teacher, still, and he had confidence in Donal's judgement. Right now, he was curious, what Donal would recommend about these happenings in the previous lives of Aiden and Callahan.

"You know, Aiden, I know, that you have prepared yourself for the confrontation with Callahan. You know that he has played a very unpleasant role in your and your mother's previous lives and that you felt and still feel right about having killed him for what he has done. I can fully understand your actions, believe me that", Donal said, and after another short pause, he continued: "You have your wooden stick and you have your two knifes, which you are thinking about to use now, to kill Callahan again – as he deserves it for being so unpleasant to you and your mother again, right?"

"Yes, right. And I appreciate your open and frank talking, Donal. Are you about to talk me out of it now?", Aiden assumed.

Donal made a sigh. "No, not really, Aiden. I am a strong believer in self-responsibility as you know. I believe that it will be your decision, finally, and that is totally acceptable for me, of course. On the other hand, I believe, I should have you sit down with me and Ide and Bridget, here, with a cup of tea, to make you think about what you are going to do. In fact – if we all are honest – we all know that Callahan is still a swine with a rotten character, there is no doubt about it at all. But, if we continue to look honestly on our current situation, all he did so far to you was to push you out of his cabin and to expel you from his land. He did not kill or rape anyone, this time – yet. Right?"

Aiden thought about it, then he said: "Yes, right."

"So, do you think it is appropriate to kill him for his push then?", Donal asked Aiden.

"I know, what you mean, Donal, but I am upset and full of rage, when I think about, what he has done to me before, do you understand that, Donal?", Aiden asked.

"I understand you, Aiden. Completely", Bridget said. "I also was in the whorehouse and Callahan raped me. Perhaps, you have recognized me there, right? And at the time I found out about it, I also wanted to kill Callahan, at first. And I still hate him and his dirty friends here in Galway. They are disgusting. But – I have learned to accept, that although we know, what he did, Callahan does not remember. He has only his limited mind, his stupidity, his greed and his rotten character. But he has no idea, why he is such a prick!", Bridget said.

"Yes, and it was me to make Bridget think about all this, when she found out about it and tried to hunt the mayor down with a knife, a couple of years ago", Donal continued.

"Yes, and now, you want to talk me out of it, I see", Aiden concluded with a smile. "That is very kind of you and I really appreciate your concern, but I will stay prepared as I know Callahan's rotten soul now and I will be ready to take his live, whenever it seems necessary for me to do it. There is no talking me out of this, believe me."

"And you also know about the karma thing. I am sure, you are fully aware, and we do not have to mention that either, Aiden, right?", Donal added calmly.

"Yes, I have thought about that too. My karma is already bad after these two murders, at least I stay on my course", Aiden replied.

"Let me just ask of you, Aiden, that you might continue to think about all that and do not act out of an impulse, you might regret. If you do something bad, you have an eternal span of time to correct it. I just think, it is better to avoid some stupid actions and to avoid bad karma before it arises. You get better rewards then and earlier. It is worth to think about it. You can break a stick in two pieces in a second, but it takes years to grow a new one for you, please remember that, when you try to act out of an impulse. Sometimes we need fast actions – ask Ide - when she grabbed your hand quickly and prevented you to fall from the cliffs into your certain death. And sometimes we need to think first and maybe skip our actions for some higher values. No one says it is easy. At least, it is good to have you back, Aiden. Now let us celebrate your arrival and talk about other things, right?", Donal said.

"Yes. Thank you for your concerns. Maybe I will think about it", Aiden said with a smile.

The Cave

Cassidy entered the room of the central building, when all magicians and students sat at the table for dinner. Although everyone could hear it, she said to Donal: "Donal, we have someone in Galway, who is a descendent from the Templars. Colin is his name. I have talked to him and he confirmed that he had heard about the treasure from his grandfather and father. Although he does not know exactly, where this treasure might be, he is willing to join us in an expedition to search for it."

"That is promising news, Cassidy. Thank you for your investigation in that case!", Donal said.

"And – ", Cassidy continued, "I have also found someone who is familiar with the caves in our area around Galway. Finn is his name. I also talked with him and he said he knows quite some caves here, but only one of them is somewhat unexplored, so he could imagine finding something inside, which he had not already discovered. It sounded promising to me, so I also invited him for a meeting to discuss an expedition to this specific cave, he has in mind."

"That sounds also very promising. Maybe we have a chance with these two gentlemen to really find this ancient treasure of the Templars", Donal said and nodded contently.

Aiden asked: "Now what? While I was not here, you started investigations to look for the Templars' treasure here in Galway? And nobody told me about it? Can I also join in?", Aiden asked.

"Of course, Aiden. You should also be part of our expedition team. I had hoped you would be interested", Donal agreed and tapped Aiden on the shoulder.

This night, betrayal came over the magicians, out of their own lines. A dark shadow could be seen stepping through the school area's door in the wall, heading for the town of Galway.

The shape went fast through the dark, looking for pursuers. As the figure reached the town, it entered the house of Sheila, Ciara's mother.

"I have news for you, mother!", Ciara said to Sheila, who was sitting in front of the fire, cleaning her dirty fingernails with her mouth, spitting the dirt on the floor.

"Ah, what is it, Ciara?", Sheila asked curiously.

"Donal wants to build a team and they want to go on an expedition to a cave, where they believe a treasure might be hidden", Ciara revealed.

"What a reliable snitch you are, my daughter! That will bring us great wealth, when we steal the treasure out of the hands of these clueless fools. Hi hi hi…", Sheila laughed like a witch with an evil plan.

Then she advised her daughter to return to the school and keep close contact to extract closer information about the expedition, where it was targeted to and when it would start. The more she knew, the better she could interfere to steal the treasure. She had imagined chests full of gold and gemstones and could not sleep that night as she had to think about how she would proceed to gain this incredible wealth for herself.

A few days later Colin and Finn came to the school for the meeting about the expedition. They sat together in the central building and Finn laid a map on the table. "If I understood you correctly, Cassidy", Finn started to talk, "then the most likely place, where I would assume any hidden treasure, is here, in this cave." Finn pointed with his finger on the map and numerous curious pairs of eyes looked at the map.

"That is not too far away from here", Donal said. "If we build our team and start tomorrow morning with our approach to the cave, we should arrive there during the day. Then, Finn, what would you think, how long might us the cave take to investigate it?", Donal asked.

"Well, that is hard to say. If we assume, that we have sections that might be hard to access, if we have to remove stones or create our way into some sections, that might take quite some days. We should be prepared for a longer stay, I would recommend, at least to have water and food for a couple of days. With that, we are on the safe side, however things develop", Finn recommended.

"Yes, that sounds good to me", Donal agreed. "Okay, then who do we have in the team? As far as I know it is you, Finn, as our cave specialist, you, Colin, as our representative for the Templars, which I believe is important as it is still property of the Order of Templars in my perspective and we do not intend to steal it", Donal explained.

"Appreciated, Donal", Colin said.

"Then Aiden wants to join as he is the successor of Owen, his father, who was involved in our expedition activities before, and we should have Ide in the team as she might be able to help with the dwarfs, we expect to meet there too. Anyone else?", Donal summarized.

"I want to join in also!", Ciara said with a loud voice. "I can help you with the stones as I have some very effective spells to move earth, dirt and obstacles of all kind!"

"Agreed. Great, then we have our team!", Donal said.

"What about you, Donal, and Cassidy? Will you not join us?", Aiden wanted to know.

"I would rather stay at the school with Cassidy. I do not like narrow caves in my age, really, and together with Cassidy, we can do important work here, rather. Although I am very curious about the outcome of that expedition, I will let the experience of this adventure to you younger folks", Donal said with a smile on his face.

Ciara went out again this night to snitch on the magicians by visiting her mother under the protection of darkness and she showed Sheila the location of the cave, as she had spied it from the map Finn had shown.

"When they have found the treasure it will be important, that we get it in our hands, Ciara. I will be there to help you, I promise. When you have a chance to act on our purpose do not wait for me, Ciara. We do not know, how difficult or easy it will be to steal the gold. We must take any chance, we get. Have you understood that?", Sheila asked her daughter.

"I am not stupid, mother. You will see, I can tear the gold out of their hands without them knowing what happened. I already have a plan", said Ciara. "And now I have to return to grab some sleep before we get on our journey tomorrow."

Aiden got up early in the morning as he was impatient to go on the expedition with the others. He checked his package again and thought about, what he might want to take with him besides the clothes, food and water. He looked at the wooden stick and although he was not sure if he would need it, as he did not expect to meet Callahan on the journey, he decided to use the stick as a walking stick. And he would also take the two knifes with him. He attached them to his belt - one on the left and one on the right side of it. He also had his fire glove in his package as it would not hurt to be able to create some fire for the night or for the dinner.

Then the team gathered in the central school building and after a short introduction to the day's tasks ahead, they said goodbye to those, who remained at the school and started their journey to the cave.

In the early afternoon they arrived at the cave. It was quite dark in it at it seemed to have no end as the tunnels were impressively long.

"Let us have a short rest here before we enter the cave and let us prepare some torches. We will need them, once we are deeper inside", Finn recommended. Then he continued: "Last time I was here, I already drew a map of the cave's tunnels, as far as I was able to explore them. That will help us to decide, which way to turn, once we are in. And it might also be an indicator to us, where we might suspect some hidden tunnels as well."

"And what about the dwarfs, Ide?", Aiden asked. "Do you remember what the fairy said? Will you tell me when they are visible to you?" Ide knew that Aiden was concerned about the fairy's talking that he should be ready to die if he wanted to proceed to the treasure.

"Sure, I will. There is no need to be worried", Ide said calmly.

"Last time, when I was here, there was no dwarf, believe me that!", Finn said with a smile. "You should not believe everything people say."

"We will see", added Ide.

After the short rest, the team entered the cave. Finn guided them through the tunnels, and they carefully inspected every wall for signs about any possible hidden tunnel or room. The deeper they came, the darker it was, and they had to use the torches, Finn had brought with him. Then, Colin noticed a sign on a wall. It was a little cross. "Look here!", he said to the others. "This little cross on the wall looks like a sign of the Templars. I am sure, that is a hint, that we will find something behind this wall. Let us try to remove the stones!", he recommended to the others.

Finn also inspected the wall and confirmed: "Yes, this wall does not look natural. If you look closer, you can see that it was built with small and big stones. It is artificial, I would say."

"Okay, then – Ciara, can you remove the wall for us with your magic expertise?", asked Aiden.

"To be honest, I cannot", admitted Ciara. "I was curious and wanted to be on this expedition, but I cannot really remove these stones. Sorry. I did not believe we would find anything interesting either."

"Wow, great", Aiden complained. Then he took his wooden stick and tried to use it as a lever against some of the stones. After he had laid a small stone under the stick and placed it below a bigger stone of the wall, he finally succeeded to move a first small part of the wall with his stick. That encouraged him and he continued to work on the wall – until finally, the first stone was set free and a tiny hole was visible on the bottom of this artificial wall. Aiden tried to look inside, but it was too dark behind the wall. So, he continued to work on the hole. A second stone got loose and was removed, then the wall was torn down faster and faster. All hands worked together, and the loosened stones were taken away and placed in some distance to the hole, which was now big enough to climb through.

"Who wants to go first?", Aiden asked. "Colin, would you like to take the first step inside? As our representative for the Templars?"

"Sure, why not", said Colin. He took a torch from Finn and climbed in. "Wow, there is a chest!", the team heard him say. Ciara was curious and could not wait, so she climbed into the hole too. "Wow, a treasure chest! Open it, open it, quick!", she asked from Colin.

As there was no lock at the chest, Colin could open it easily and the gold in the chest sparkled and shone in the light of the torch.

"Wow, we are rich!" shouted Ciara. "We got it! Yeah!"

"Okay", said Finn, "let us try to move the chest through the hole to get it out. Then we can inspect it if there is something else in it too."

Ciara grabbed one side of the chest and pulled it hard, Colin helped her, and they succeeded to pull the chest to the hole and then pushed it outside to the team. Then Ciara and Colin climbed out of the small room, back into the tunnel, where the others stood.

As they had all looked inside the chest and had seen all the gold in it, Colin said: "That was too easy. That was somehow the style of the Templars to have a sign on the wall to mark the place, where the chest was hidden, but I believe, there might be more in this cave than just this chest of gold. It is just a feeling. I cannot explain it, I just think, as I knew my grandfather, I think, there might be more."

"Ah, I am bored and tired", Ciara complained. "If you want to move on into the cave, then go. I will stay here and have a break instead. When you come back with empty hands, we can leave the cave together. Sounds like a plan, yes?"

"I believe Colin is right. There might be more to be found. I would like to continue the search. Those who want to continue, come with us, the rest might wait here, okay?", Aiden proposed.

Ciara was the only one of the team, who wanted to stay, the others agreed to continue to search and go deeper into the cave. Ciara smiled. She was about to succeed with her plan, just a few moments and then it would be done!

As the team walked on deeper into the cave, Ciara concentrated her mind and let the ceiling of the cave collapse. Stones fell into the tunnel with a loud noise and dust filled the air. The team was locked in and could not come after her, when she would escape with the gold!

"Oh my god, oh my god! You all will die! Oh my god!", shouted Ciara, hoping, the others would believe her the desperation she played for them.

Sheila, who had already arrived at the cave's entry heard the falling stones and Ciara's shouting. She decided to enter the cave and hoped to find Ciara with a rich treasure in there. And she did. Together Ciara and Sheila took the chest and left the team enclosed in the tunnels, where these would die while those were rich.

Finn could not believe it. "How could that happen?", he asked surprised. "I have been in so many caves, these caves are hundreds of years old or older and why does it collapse at the time, when we are right here? One of you is cursed! I have no other explanation. And I think it is you, Colin. You touched the treasure first, so maybe the curse of the Templars came over you! Or it is you, Aiden. You have removed the wall with the cross! One of you is cursed! Damn it, damn it!"

"Maybe it is even you, Finn", Colin replied, "cussing on everything."

"Maybe we should all calm down and work on a rescue plan instead, how about that?", Ide asked.

"Yes, you are right, Ide. Complaining does not help. We should try to find out, what options we have and then decide, how we will proceed. Removing these massive stones here will not work, that much is certain", Aiden concluded.

"When I look on my map, there are quite some tunnels, we have not yet explored deeper, we could try to find another escape at the end of one of those tunnels, how does that sound?", Finn asked.

"When I look on your map, Finn, I would not know, where to start. It could take us hours, our torches will burn down, and we will be stuck in the darkness, if we fail", Aiden feared.

"We have another chance", Ide said, "Show me the map, please, Finn." As Finn handed the map to Ide, she looked at it carefully and concentrated. "What is this – here? The circle here on the map, what is it?" she asked.

"This is water in one of the tunnels. I have marked it on the map as I did not want to get wet again when I would come back a second time. First time I fell into this waterhole when I slipped on the wet floor", Finn explained.

"Okay, that might be our chance", Ide continued, "let us go to the waterhole then and see if we can find someone there!"

"Are you sick?", asked Finn, "Who should be there? We are under the earth. Nobody will be there. Nobody was there last time. It is far too deep in the tunnels!"

"Have a little trust", Aiden proposed, as he had an idea, what Ide expected at the waterhole.

After a short walk through the tunnels and due to the exact map of Finn, the group finally arrived at the waterhole.

"Sit down and rest, please", Ide asked from the others. Then she also sat down and looked at the water, the torch in her hand. "Hello", she said softly. "May I please speak with one of you? – Hello? Please, would you please talk to me?"

Nothing happened.

"I told you, there is nobody here! You see now?", Finn said frustrated.

"Shut up", Ide said and then calmed down and added "please. Sorry for my tone, Finn. I just try to make contact with an elf or more likely with a dwarf. So please let me try and be silent for a while, will you?"

Suddenly a stone fell from the ceiling and crashed into the waterhole. Then they heard a voice: "What do you want? Have you come to destroy the cave? You will die herein! All of you! This is, what you deserve!", the angry voice said.

"Oh please, no", Ide said calmly, "we came here because we wanted to explore the cave. We have no intention to destroy anything. Stones fell down and have locked us in. And now, we simply try to find a way out. We do not want to die herein, you see?"

"But you will die! If you lie, you will die! Do you hear me?", the angry voice asked.

"Yes, of course, I can hear you. Please, you can investigate my heart, I know that. Look and see that I speak the truth. We are trying to survive, and that is the reason, why we came to this waterhole – to talk to you and ask for your help. To find a way out of these tunnels.", Ide explained again.

"You came to steal! I know that! You came to steal, and you will die here in the cave! That's it! Now die silently you cowards!", the angry voice shouted. Then a strong breeze went through the tunnels and all the torches went out.

"Damn it! I knew it! You are cursed! Damn it!", Ide heard, and she knew that was Finn, again.

Total darkness surrounded the group, there was no light at all. They were locked in the tunnel and the only thing they could sense was the sound of their breaths. Then there was another soft sound. Someone was rummaging in his backpack.

"Ah, here it is, finally!" Ide heard Aiden's voice. Then she saw a bubble of light, no, it was a fireball in Aiden's hand. He had searched for the leather glove in his backpack, had put it on and then created the fireball to light the torches again.

As the first torch burnt again, the fireball disappeared.

"Wow, what was that? Are you a wizard?", Colin asked.

"Magician is the right word. I am not a wizard, I am a magician", Aiden insisted.

"Who are you, boy?", Aiden heard the angry voice say.

"I am Aiden, son of Owen, sir – and who are you, if I may ask, please?", Aiden wanted to know.

"I am Root! And I am the leader of the dwarfs here in this cave. We protect these natural tunnels and the treasures in it. And you talk to fire entities, right?", asked the dwarf.

"To be honest, I am still a beginner. I had my moments, let's say, with some outcomes I am not very proud of", Aiden admitted. "We came here to search for the treasure of the Templars, which we believed might be hidden here in this cave, Root."

"And then you want to steal it! You all will die!", Root said angry again.

"We do not want to steal anything, please, believe us. We came here to explore, to see, what we can find, and we found a treasure chest behind a wall, full of gold. Then the ceiling fell down and locked us in to die. That is, why we came here for help, and that is all", Aiden explained again.

"I know you boy! You came here to destroy! You have burnt down Galway, I know that! With your fireballs in your rage! You came here to destroy and you all will die in this cave and now I will leave you alone to face your death!", Root grumbled.

"Please, Root", Ide said, "Aiden was young and did not want to burn Galway at that time. We are magicians and we live in a spirit to help each other and also to help you, the dwarfs, the elves and fairies, ghosts, lost souls, whatever you can imagine. We are good people, even as we have our mistakes, we are good people and we came in good will, please, believe us, Root."

Silence was all they got as an answer.

Ciara and Sheila managed to steal the treasure chest out of the cave, loaded it on a wagon and drove it home to Sheila's house. Then they drank wine and celebrated their success. Late in the night both fell asleep, drunken from their boozing.

In the cave the group also laid down to rest on the cold floor of the tunnel and tried to sleep a while. They had put out the torch and closed their eyes.

Aiden calmed his mind and concentrated. He had a strange feeling about being locked up in this cave, so he tried to go back in time and look for an answer about this feeling.

Then Aiden saw a group of men. They were locked in a cave; a small tunnel and dirt was all around them. It was the memory of a previous life, where he was locked up in a similar tunnel like today, with a group of men, workers. There had been an accident and the workers got caught in the tunnel. Some of them were injured from the falling stones, so was Aiden's incarnation, Frank was his name. As Frank laid in the cave, and his death was near as breathing got harder and harder, he saw the angel of death. Frank was not frightened at all, as he already thought, that they all would die in the tunnel, so he did not really care. Then he saw a dwarf at the side of the angel of death and that surprised him. The angel and the dwarf discussed, as the angel said it would not yet be time for Frank to die and the dwarf said he could offer his help, in case, Frank was worth it.

The dwarf talked with Frank then and somehow Frank managed to get the dwarfs trust. That was, when the dwarf offered to help and show the group of workers a way out of the tunnel. That was, how they survived. The name of this dwarf was Hailen.

Aiden woke up. "Root, are you there?", Aiden asked. "Do you know Hailen? He is a friend of mine. Have you heard of him?"

"Where do you know Hailen from?", Root asked softly.

"It is a long story and long ago I believe. I was locked in a tunnel once, a smaller one like this one here and Hailen helped me and my men to find a way out, alive. I am still very thankful for that", Aiden said to the dwarf.

Silence − again. And darkness. Then, after an eternity it seemed, the walls in the tunnel began to glow in a soft blue light.

Ide and Aiden saw the dwarf, standing in the tunnel in front of them. "I will help you. A friend of Hailen is a friend of me. Come, get your team together and I will show you a way out", the dwarf offered.

Ide and Aiden woke the others and told them to collect their things together as they were about to leave the cave now.

Colin and Finn were quite surprised as they saw the blue glowing walls of the tunnels. "Is this another trick?", Colin asked.

"No", Aiden said, "it is the help of a friendly dwarf. Now come, it is time to go!"

They had to walk through a couple of tunnels, sometimes they had to crawl through tiny holes and finally, the first ray of daylight hit Aiden's face. What a relief. "Climb out the cave, I will follow you, once you all made it out, okay?", Aiden proposed. Colin and Finn climbed out first, Ide stayed with Aiden, as she could also see Root and was curious, what would come now.

"Root, may I ask you a question, please?", Aiden wanted to know.

"What is it?", the dwarf said curiously.

"We came here into this cave as we have heard from a fairy, that a treasure of the Templars is hidden in one of the caves in our countryside around Galway. We thought it was this cave here and we found indeed a treasure chest, hidden behind an artificial wall, marked with a cross. Is there more than this chest of gold? We believe, there might be more. Would you mind talking about that?", Aiden asked.

"As friend of Hailen, I can tell you, yes, there is more. The chest with the gold and jewelry was only a trap for greedy thieves. The true treasure is hidden at another place in the cave and we keep it safe, believe me that", Root confirmed.

"Would you mind if we came back to have a look on this treasure, Root?", Aiden continued to ask.

"To see this treasure, Aiden, you must be willing to die. And I mean it, honestly. There is a magic spell on that treasure, and you will only survive, if your soul is clear like a flower in the sun. Something, we do not see often on this planet. If you think you are ready to die, you may come back and bring your girlfriend too, she is also welcome and can take your dead body home, if you should fail the test", Root explained.

A shiver ran down Aiden's back. He had not expected such clear and frank words, but he was thankful for that. At least he knew now that there was a chance to see the true treasure of the Templars. Once he would be ready to die. For today, Aiden was not sure about this yet.

"Thank you, Root, for your frank answer and your willingness to safe our lives today. We will always remember that kindness. Thank you", Aiden said again.

"Thank you very much, Root, and goodbye", Ide added.

Then they climbed out of the cave and Colin asked: "What took you so long?"

"We had to put the blue light out first and did not know, how that was done. Now we know.", Aiden said.

"You are kidding us, yes?", Finn wanted to know.

"Yes, we are kidding. We wanted to have a moment for ourselves in that romantic cave", Aiden said, looked to Ide and his head once again turned red.

Ide shook her head. "Yeah, he is so horny sometimes", she said and smiled.

Aiden did not know, what he should say now. The situation was absolutely embarrassing to Aiden, yet he felt somehow responsible for that, too.

Reflections

After the group had returned safely to Galway with empty hands, Ciara came to the table, where Ide and Aiden were sitting for breakfast, next morning.

"Oh, my dear, you are alive!", Ciara said and showed a surprised behavior. "I thought you all were dead. You know, as the stones came down, I was so lucky, that I was not hit by them. The treasure chest got completely covered by these heavy stones, when they had fallen, and I was so frightened. There was no sign of life from you all, so I decided to return to Galway without you. I really believed that you all had died."

"We could escape, fortunately. We also thought that we would have to die in the tunnels", Ide explained. "It was not easy, but finally, we were able to get back to daylight." She sensed that something was wrong and could not say if it was, because Ciara had a bad conscience about what happened or if she was not fully honest about her feelings. Ide remained polite while she kept her suspicious thoughts for herself.

After the breakfast, Aiden went to Ide, looked around to make sure nobody was listening, and started talking: "Ide, can I ask you something, please? When we climbed out of the cave and you made this remark about me, being horny sometimes – you know, that felt totally embarrassing to me. Why did you say that?"

"Oh, Aiden", Ide replied to him, "I did not mean to hurt you with that comment. I am sorry. You know – I have noticed that you currently develop your sexual sensitivity, which is totally normal for a young man of your age. And I just wanted to make a funny statement about it, not more. To me, sexuality is something incredibly special and at the same time very natural, and I can imagine, that it is not easy for you to find your way to deal with it. That might be the reason, why you felt embarrassed by my comment. I am terribly sorry. Sometimes, we get ourselves in the middle of some trouble when we try to be funny and do not think about the consequences. I really did not mean it, believe me, Aiden", Ide apologized.

"Yes, do not worry, Ide. I was simply confused. I have these sexual feelings, they come suddenly, when I find myself attracted by you or Bridget and I cannot do anything against it. It is as if something takes control over some parts of me. I do not know, how to explain that, really", Aiden said.

"You know what, Aiden – let us talk about sexuality. That might not hurt, I think. How is it for you? How does it feel to you, when you get attracted by a woman?", Ide wanted to know from Aiden.

"Well, that is feeling so strange to me to talk about it, really. But I know you so well, so I will try, Ide. When I see you or Bridget, sometimes, it is – how do I say that – it is a strong desire rising inside of me and I would like to touch your skin, to feel you and – ah, yes, many other things. I think you know, what I mean. I am once again feeling uncomfortable to talk about it. It is not easy", Aiden admitted.

"Yes, I fully understand that, Aiden", Ide replied. "Let me explain something to you then: Sexuality is part of our human life, it is something that drives us and you can say, nature itself implanted our sexual desire into us to make sure, that we, and all living beings, would have an interest to reproduce ourselves, so that our kind, our species continues through and with our children. It is a natural power and it has indeed something to do with our spiritual energies. Now that is the reason why so many people have problems with their sexuality. They do not understand what love is, they do not understand their sexuality and the difference between love and sex. And as the sexual energy can drive a person hard, a lot of people cannot control this energy, and that can really be problematic. – You remember your life as a prostitute, I know. How did you feel when the sailors came to you for sex?"

"That was a mix of feelings, to be honest. First, I felt insecure to be part in something, that I could not fully control. And when you then get touched by someone you barely know, it is – now how can I explain that – it is somehow frightening, because there is no trust, you do not know, what this person does with you, and then I felt used. Like a thing or so. I felt not to be fully integrated in the situation, it was, as if I only were partially in the situation and other important parts of myself were outside the process – to protect myself, you can say. I could not really enjoy the sexual experience itself, and after it, I felt dirty and wanted to wash my body. But even after washing my body, there have been things in my mind, that I could not wash away. That was something I had to learn to deal with. I think, I built a kind of distance between myself and all these men. A mental barrier to somehow protect my feelings. Otherwise, I am certain, I would have been broken in the process. It was not easy for me", Aiden explained.

"Yes, for me it was similar. Finally, if you really want to enjoy your sexuality, it is as you mentioned: There should be a mutual trust, you should know each other and if you love each other, then it gets magical. If it is just about the physical activity, the touching and the stimulations of the body, that does not really fulfill you in the long run. If there is trust and loving, that brings an intimacy that makes your sexual experience something beautiful and worthful. One day, I am certain about that, you will find out, how that feels, Aiden. And if everything is right, then it is wonderful", said Ide.

"I would be so happy, if I could have my first sexual experience with you, Ide, really. I mean in this life, now", Aiden admitted.

"Oh Aiden, I appreciate your thoughts, really. You know, if we did it, it would change your relation to Bridget, can you see that? We two, you and me, would have a new experience that could bring us closer together and on the other hand it might be the case, that you lose a part of your relationship to Bridget. Now, today, you are a friend to both of us, then, you would be the lover of one of us and that would make a difference to the other one, can you see that? Now the question is – do you really want that? Do you really want to change the relationship between us three? If you are honest, Aiden, I believe you could also have a sexual experience with Bridget, and this would also be okay. And the relationship between us, you and me, would then somehow change as a result. To have a good friend has a special worth, Aiden, and if you ask me, I would not want to lose any part of our intimacy and relationship and I would not like to exchange it for a sexual experience with you, Aiden. I would rather like to appreciate what we have and to keep it alive, as it is. A pure and innocent friendship where we can talk about everything, and I really mean everything. We have no reason to hurt each other, we do not even have a reason to think that some of our actions or words could hurt the other, as we are friends and not lovers. A sexual experience changes a relationship, you will see that, when it happens, and maybe you can imagine it with your knowledge from your previous lives, Aiden", Bridget explained.

"Yes, I think, I understand, what you mean. And, indeed, if I should choose between you and Bridget, I do not know, if I could do it right. I could not say, which choice would be the right one or let me say, both choices seem so right, that it is impossible to decide between you and Bridget. Yes, somehow, both of you are of highest worth to me, and if I am honest to myself, I would regret it too, if I would lose any part of our current intimacy and relationship", Aiden admitted.

"Now we must live with our challenges then, I guess. When we get tempted we must struggle with ourselves to protect the intimacy, we all share with each other, rather than to give ourselves in to a sudden situation, which might cause changes to some of the valuable things we have", Ide said.

"Yes, I see it now. That was good talking to you, Ide, really. Now I feel much more confident about my sexuality and I believe I will not get embarrassed next time, when one of us talks about anything related to sex again. At least I hope so", Aiden concluded.

Ide smiled and gave Aiden a hug.

Later the day, Ide and Aiden asked Donal for a talk. "May we have a word with you, Donal?", Ide asked.

"Yes, sure, come in my room", Donal proposed, and Ide and Aiden followed him to his study room, where Donal often kept his privacy to do some research, meditation or investigations of different kinds. "What can I do for you?", he asked.

"When we were in the cave with the dwarf, Donal, before we climbed back to the surface, we had a short talk with this dwarf, Root is his name. He told us, that there is a hidden treasure of the Templars in the cave, besides the chest of gold that we had found, and he invited Aiden and me to come back, when we are ready, to have a look on it", Ide explained to Donal.

"That is remarkably interesting news, Ide. It is also my feeling, that the Templars had more than only gold with them, when they arrived in 1307. At least we have now better knowledge, where this treasure is hidden", concluded Donal.

"What I do not understand", Aiden started, "is, when the Templars came to Galway and we have people like Colin, the grandson of a Templar, how does it come, that the treasure is still hidden in the cave and where are these Templars today? I mean the rest of them. Have they disappeared?", Aiden wanted to know.

"I do not know exactly, what happened then", Donal answered. "From what I know, the Templars decided to go on a journey with their ship, some of the Templars remained in Galway, like the grandfather of Colin and a few others. The rest went somewhere, I do not know where, and they did not come back, as far as it is known. As those that stayed here had been waiting for the return of their fellows, I believe, over time, the treasure's location was somehow forgotten or even never known to those, who stayed in Galway", Donal explained.

"Now, what would you recommend, what should we do? Root invited Ide and me to come back to the cave. As Colin is not invited and we consider him the rightful descendent of the Templars, is it okay, if we go there without him to have a look at the treasure? Would that not be a kind of betrayal?", Aiden wanted to know from Donal.

"Look, Aiden. The dwarf oversees the treasure's protection. When Root decided to invite you and Ide only, I would say, if you take Colin with you, it would be a betrayal of the dwarf. So, I think it is okay, if you both return to the cave and we can inform Colin later, once we know more. We do not have an intention to hide or steal something from Colin, that is the most important point. Anything else can be decided later as long as we keep being honest and open to answer frankly to Colin about everything, he might ask. I think it is okay, if you go there if you want", Donal concluded.

"Okay Donal, thank you for your opinion. It will help us to decide, once we know, what we would like to do", Ide said.

"Can I have a word with you both, in private, please?", Aiden asked, as he met Bridget and Ide next morning in the school's area. "Would you mind following me to a quiet room, please?"

"Sure, anytime", Bridget said, and Ide nodded. They went to the main school building and sat together in a room privately.

"You know", Aiden started, "that I had this life in the whorehouse as Penny, and you both have been there too. From your experience, is that normal, that those connections happen or is it just a huge coincidence that we have met in this ancient life before? How would you see that?"

"Well", Bridget started, "as I see it, we are connected. Our souls have a connection that lasts for several lives, for centuries, maybe forever. When we decide, as a soul, to have a life experience on earth, or somewhere else, we also decide, if we want to have this experience together with friends, with souls, that we already know. That is quite natural. And so, it is completely normal, that we meet each other again and again, in different roles, with different physical connections on earth, if you want. As friends, as siblings, as parent and child and so on. To me, that is fully understandable and that is, what I learned from my own experience, when I looked into my previous lives."

"Yes, I fully agree", Ide said. "This is also my experience and knowledge. If we have a connection with each other, then this connection can last and span a couple of lives. It may even be, that groups of souls stay together, that is quite normal. On the other hand, it does also make sense to meet new souls, to change the environment, to go out for new experiences, so it is absolutely possible and normal, that we meet souls, we have never met before. It is like an ocean, we are taken up into the sky by the sunlight, we drop down from a cloud as a raindrop and we may gather in a single puddle on earth. Or we may fall on separate plants or animals and get lost from each other. But the day will come when we find our way back into the ocean. That is, how I would explain that."

"That is very interesting. And karma influences, what kind of experience we will have, based on that, what we have created for others. And now – if it comes to those souls like that of Callahan or Glen-Bill, those creatures, that we really dislike – why don't we get rid of them? Why do we also meet them over and over? Why can souls like Callahan's not disappear and leave us alone?", Aiden asked.

"You should try to see the big picture, Aiden", Ide continued. "We are here to learn. Once we do someone harm, then this creates a connection to this soul, that we have hurt. If we want it or not. We create a connection and karma takes care, that our souls get back into a natural balance, in harmony. When the other soul pays us back in the same or next life, the connection gets even stronger. And so – by time – things develop in both directions. Our connections to our friends and our connections to the souls, that we hurt and that hurt us, get stronger. That is a natural effect. If you ask me, Aiden, if you want to get rid of Callahan's soul, you have to forgive him, what he did to you. All of it. All of it! That is the only chance, I believe."

"I am not sure, if I can do that", Aiden honestly replied.

"Yes, that is, why we are always here, bound to each other, if we like it or not. There are some things I cannot forgive either", Bridget added, "and I do not even know if I want to learn to forgive. It is as it is, and I always try to make the best out of it. As long as I feel okay with what I do, it is okay. At least for me. Sounds hard, can be hard. It is my life and my journey." After a short pause, Bridget added: "And I am very happy to have some friends like you!"

"Even if I get horny again?", Aiden asked.

"Even then", Bridget and Ide said, like with one voice and they smiled.

"You are great. I love you both!", Aiden admitted.

In the evening, Aiden thought again about these connections of souls. He knew that he had an old connection with his mother's soul, as she had already been his mother in his life as Navin in India and now again. He also knew that he had connections to Bridget and Ide from his life as Penny in the whorehouse. From his life as Frank in the cave he knew not much yet, only that his experience with the dwarf Hailen had saved his life, twice now.

The only thing, that disturbed Aiden was the connection to Callahan's soul. Was Aiden responsible for the start of this enduring connection to such an ugly soul, as it was his action to kill the rapist in India in the first step? Was that the beginning of this unpleasant connection? But what could he have done instead? Should he just accept, that this fat rich man raped his mother and insulted him again and again and then do nothing about it? Aiden felt right about killing the rapist in India and again in the whorehouse. The killing was well deserved, and Aiden was not willing to accept everything, just to not get into a connection with an unpleasant soul.

Maybe that was the reason: In a paradise, there would only be harmony and love – no challenge to get upset or angry, and so no chance to learn about anger and hate, too. Now what was better? To constantly live in harmony and peace or the experience of all these kinds of feelings, and in order to complete the picture, to also feel the bad things, hate, anger, embarrassment, pain, whatever? Which way would be better?

Life is, as it is, Aiden thought. We have to experience good and bad situations, and that will never change. We only can choose to learn from it.

And then, with all our knowledge, we can try to find the best way to deal with it, for ourselves. And from that perspective, it seemed quite inevitable to Aiden to get good as well as bad connections, to souls that you like and to those that you dislike.

You simply have to live with that. It is a constant challenge. Aiden decided for himself, to deal with any situation between himself and Callahan, as it might feel right in that moment, and to not take care about the karmic relationships or connections it might establish or strengthen. Just live and decide for the right thing to do, in every moment. Do not make plans, simply live and act out of the situation. Could that be so hard?

When night was laying down over Galway and it was time to sleep, Aiden still could not find peace of mind. He had the feeling, he should investigate his life as Frank, when he was locked into the cave with his workers. What was the reason for this accident there, how did they get locked in and more importantly – and that was a terrible suspicion that struck Aiden – had Callahan something to do with it, too?

Aiden laid on his bed, closed his eyes and went back in time, as he had done several times before. He went directly to his life as Frank, the miner. As he looked closely into the happenings of this life, Aiden slowly began to understand. Frank's task was to dig for iron ore when they had found a gold vein one day. The iron ore could be won with straight tunnels, but to mine the gold, they would have to dig upwards, with the risk that the tunnels might fall in and get flooded by the water of a lake above the tunnels. Frank, the soul of Aiden, was the foreman of these workers and he talked about his concerns with the boss of this enterprise. But the boss was a greedy man, people only called him Grunt, as he snored heavily in his sleep, and it sounded like a pig. This greedy man demanded from Frank and his workers to dig upwards to get hands on the gold. He did not respect the risk these workers had to bear. As this greedy man could not wait for the gold, which came in slowly every day, he decided to use dynamite to work the tunnels faster into the height, where the gold was in the walls. Then – one day – as the greedy man caused an explosion, Frank and his workers got locked in, as the tunnels collapsed. That was, when Frank and his workers were sentenced to death, would the dwarf Hailen not have helped them to survive.

As Aiden returned from his meditation into the presence of his room in Galway, he knew, that this greedy man in that life was the soul of Callahan. Again. It was no surprise to Aiden and slowly but surely, he got really sick of that man.

Revenge

Dark clouds gathered in the evening sky as if heaven knew, what the evil witch Sheila was about to do. When she was informed by her daughter Ciara that the others had safely returned from the cave, she felt it would be too dangerous to return to the cave and perhaps get discovered by the magicians at the attempt to find more treasure chests. So, she decided to send someone else to the cave instead of going there herself.

Sheila left her house and walked through the streets of Galway to visit her assistant – and this should be Callahan, the mayor. She knocked on the door and before someone could answer, she stepped into the mayor's house.

"Callahan, are you here? I have great news for you!", Sheila started talking.

"What do you want?", a voice replied from the other room, then Callahan appeared. "What is so important, that you cannot wait for me to open the door?", he said unfriendly.

"I know, where treasures of gold are hidden not far away from here! And I want to offer you the chance to get rich by simply grabbing this gold!", Sheila announced.

"And why would you tell me that and not grab the gold yourself?", Callahan asked curiously.

"That is easy to explain", Sheila said and sat down at the table. "Ciara, my daughter has been on an expedition with some magicians from the school and then they have found a treasure chest, full with gold, in a cave, not far from Galway", Sheila said, as she pulled a golden coin from her pocket and laid it on the table to demonstrate the truth of her words. "Unfortunately, this chest was taken by the magicians", Sheila lied. "As you can imagine, if Ciara and myself go to that cave to search for more gold, it would mean real trouble for Ciara and she might be expelled from the school, if we get caught in the act. You, on the other hand, as the mayor, would have no reason to explain yourself to the magicians if they meet you in the cave. You can simply threaten them away. Am I right?"

"How much gold is there in the cave?", Callahan asked and tried to grab the coin on the table, but Sheila was quicker and pulled it back into her pocket before he could touch it.

"Enough. More than you can imagine!", Sheila exaggerated. "In the cave there are tunnels, lots of tunnels, and on the walls, there are small signs of a cross, and behind those signs there are treasure chests full of gold and jewels. Ciara has seen it and was able to grab the golden coin that I have shown to you."

"And now you come and want me to get rich?", Callahan asked. "Why should I believe you? Why would you do that?"

"Because I will get eighty percent of the gold, that you will find as my reward for telling you where this cave is", Sheila explained.

Callahan started to laugh: "You dirty crazy witch! I could kill you easily as soon as I know, where this cave is. Are you insane? Eighty percent! I will give you ten percent! I have the risk, I have the work, ten percent is more than you deserve!"

"Okay, then let it be. Then I go back, and you can forget all I have said. I will deny having ever been here and I will no longer say anything about the gold to anyone", Sheila said sulky and stood up from the table.

"Wait!", Callahan said and grabbed her hand. "I'll give you twenty percent!"

"Sixty!", Sheila haggled.

"Not more than thirty percent or I will find a reason to put you in the torture chamber!", Callahan threatened her.

"Okay, thirty percent and no tricks or I will put a spell on you and your relatives!", Sheila threatened him back.

"Okay, agreed. Where is the cave?", Callahan wanted to know. Sheila turned back to the table and sat down again. Then she pulled a map from her clothes and presented the cave's location to Callahan.

"You should not wait too long to collect the gold. I know that the magicians are eager to collect it too and there is no time to lose, if we want to safe what is left in the cave for ourselves!", Sheila said impatiently.

"Let this be my concern and now let me alone!", Callahan demanded.

Two days later Aiden and Ide returned to the cave to meet with Root and ask for permission to see the Templar's hidden treasure. They brought a wagon with them, just in case, there would be something to transport back to the school. And they once again had some food and water to supply themselves, in case, they would stay longer than expected. They placed the wagon under some trees and took care, that the horse was fed well and that it had enough to drink until they would return. Then Ide and Aiden walked towards the cave's entrance.

Suddenly they stopped. "Do you see that?", Aiden asked. "There is someone at the cave's entrance!"

"Yes, I see that, and it is not Root. It is a huge human. Let us get closer to see, if we know him", Ide proposed, and they continued their way to the cave.

As they were close to the entrance, Aiden was shocked. "It is Callahan! I don't believe it!", Aiden said surprised. Then he ran to the cave's entry as fast as he could and as he was near enough, he asked him directly: "Callahan, what do you do here?"

Ide was desperate. How could Aiden be so unreasonable and speak to Callahan directly? They should have waited and watched what was going on instead of intervening so suddenly. But is was too late for that.

Callahan turned around and yelled to Aiden: "The lousy boy! Again! Go away and let me alone! This is now my cave and no one else will enter here as long as I am here. Go back, where you came from. I will come and draw you to punishment later for the fire you have caused in Galway. I have not forgotten what you did, and I will never forgive you that! Now get out! If you do not listen to me, you will regret it sooner than you like it!"

Aiden took a deep breath as he stood in front of Callahan and took both his knifes out of the belt. In each hand he firmly held a knife and then he said to the fat mayor: "No, Callahan, now you listen to me. You have pushed me out of your cabin into the rain when thunder and flashes frightened me. You have expelled me from your land, while I was not doing anything bad. You have threatened my mother and you have searched me for years to punish me for the fire, that only started because of you. Now here I am. And here it ends. Now and forever!" And after a few seconds, Aiden added: "I forgive you!", and Aiden let the knifes fall to the earth, to Callahan's feet, as he wanted to finish the karmic connection between them once and for all.

"But I do not forgive you, lousy boy!", Callahan shouted, then grabbed the knifes from the floor and jumped towards Aiden. With all his strength he stuck the blades into Aidens sides, where the kidneys are. Aiden opened his mouth and without a sound he fell to the ground. Blood spread out slowly but constantly building a dark and growing puddle on the ground.

Callahan showed no further interest in Aiden, turned around and stepped into the cave to search for the gold.

Ide was shocked as she saw how Aiden was hurt by Callahan. She ran to Aiden and found him with both knifes still sticking in his sides. Blood came out of the body's wounds and Aiden had lost his consciousness.

Aiden saw himself, standing beside his bleeding body. Then he felt a cold breeze in his back and turned around. The angel of death was here, and Aiden was frightened, but not as much, as he was, when he had seen the angel for the first time at the cliffs. "And now?", Aiden asked.

"Now, Aiden, it is time for me to guide you to the other side. I will bring you safely home through the tunnel of light, where you will meet your beloved relatives."

"I am not prepared for that!", Aiden said. "No, that is not fair. I wanted to make peace with Callahan, and he killed me! I want to live, that is not fair!"

"Aiden, you would not believe, how many senseless discussions I already had with lots of human souls, that were not ready to die. There is no way out. Now is the time for you to be going to the other side. You will see, everything will be fine. I am here and I will stay at your side, as long as you need my company, to do, what has to come for you. As Ide said, I am your friend, and what comes now is inevitable for you, Aiden. If you want me to keep my friendly appearance you better come with me now. Come", the angel insisted and took Aiden's hand as the tunnel of light appeared in front of them.

"I guess I deserved that for killing him first", Aiden said in resignation. Slowly and constantly Aiden and the angel of death entered the tunnel.

Surprisingly, it took not very long, and Callahan found a small cross on a wall in one of the tunnels. He took the spade, he had brought here, in his hand and began to hit the wall with it. His heart pumped like hell as he hit the wall stronger and faster, again and again. Then the wall fell in. And with it, the ceiling came down and buried Callahan's fat body under heavy stones, dirt and dust.

After that, silence returned in the tunnels. Pure and peaceful silence.

Ide concentrated as she tried to reach out to Aiden's human soul to ask for Aiden's return into his physical body. But she could not contact him. No matter how desperately she tried, there was no sign of Aiden's soul. When she opened her eyes again, she saw Aiden's pale body again. Then the bleeding stopped. Aiden was gone.

Ide had tears in her eyes as she took Aiden's body over her shoulder to bring it to the wagon. It looked quite strange to see, how easily Ide carried Aiden's body as she was a delicate figure and did not make an extraordinarily strong impression. But she was determined and used her magic powers to elevate Aiden's body to return it to the school.

Finally, after hours, when she arrived at the school's area, Cassidy and Bridget helped Ide to carry Aiden's body into a small building and put it on a table there.

They all were shocked, and Bridget asked: "What happened?"

"It was Callahan. When we arrived at the cave, Callahan was there, and Aiden ran to him. It all happened so quickly, and Callahan took Aiden's knifes to slaughter him. I could not do anything to prevent it. I tried to reach out for Aiden's soul to bring him back, but I failed.", Ide said with a long sigh.

"Do not worry, Ide", Bridget tried to comfort her, as she removed the blades from Aiden's body. "Not every soul can be brought back. Sometimes it is time for them to return home and there is nothing anyone could do about it."

Then – suddenly – blood spurted again from the wounds of Aiden's body. "Look!", Bridget said. "Help me, maybe it is not yet too late!"

Cassidy took care of one wounded side while Bridget laid her hands on the other side. Ide stepped to the frontside of the table and took Aiden's head in her hands. Then all three women concentrated and imagined, how Aiden's wounds would heal. Cassidy and Bridget visualized, how Aiden's kidneys got wrapped into blue light and were supplied with a cooling paste to stop the bleeding there.

Then his kidneys got connected with orange light-cables to support them with vitalizing energy, once the bleeding would be contained. Then Cassidy and Bridget visualized how the wounds in Aiden's side got covered with a green-yellow paste of light. Finally, the belly was wrapped in a green light-bandage with golden sparks, which would remain there, until Aiden's wounds would have recovered completely.

In the meantime, Ide visualized, how Aiden's body was supplied with fresh energy from the universe, and she took care of all of Aiden's chakras, one after the other, to stimulate the healing, as slowly as necessary and as enduring as possible.

The three women saw that Aiden started breathing, slowly, weakly. He did not open his eyes yet and so they decided to stay with him and observe his condition.

Aiden was in a coma. His astral body was conscious while his physical body was sleeping. Aiden felt wonderfully comfortable and he enjoyed just being there and feeling good. Then he saw an angel and he asked him: "Hello, who are you? You are definitely not the angel of death, right?", Aiden wanted to know.

"I am your guardian angel, Aiden. And I am here to send you back to life. It is time, that you open your eyes and return to those, who love you", the angel said.

"Ah, I don't think so. Why should I? It is so good here, where I am now. To me it seems, I have all the time of the world and why should I want to hurry?", Aiden asked.

"Because your life is waiting, isn't it? You have not been born to lay in a coma, Aiden. Your purpose is to be awake and show some interest. Take part in your life and use it! What sense does it make when you stay in this condition? It does not make any sense at all! Now come on and open your eyes, Aiden!", the angel demanded.

"Why would I want to do that? Whatever I have tried, it did not really work out well. I tried to contact my father and it did not work. Then I went to the expedition with Bridget to search for Atlantis and the ship sank. Then she nearly died when she met the dragon. Could I pass the dragon to get into the cave and find out, what it protected there? No, I could not. And then I was looking for the treasure of the Templars in the cave near Galway. We found a chest with gold, but when we returned to see the true treasure, I got nearly killed by Callahan. So, you see? Nothing really worked out fine for me. Why should I want to return then? Here, I do not have any sorrow, no problems, everything is fine. Just let me rest in peace, my guardian angel, whose name I do not even know. Go - everything is fine", Aiden said.

"Oh no, nothing is fine! Aiden! You really believe, you can judge, what went right and what went wrong in your life so far? How can you dare to say that everything went wrong, and nothing worked out fine for you? Are you completely insane? Or are you not human enough to continue working on your tasks on earth? Do you really want to give yourself up? I tell you, what will happen: Your body grows older every day and when you finally feel fit to return to your life on earth, you will be an old and broken man, which was nearly killed by his enemy, Callahan, and then had never recovered from these wounds. You pity yourself. Isn't there anything in your life, that you really love? Anything, that would be worth to return for? Anything? Aiden answer me!", the angel demanded, and he sounded upset.

"I don't know", Aiden admitted.

"But I do know. Do not give yourself up, Aiden. You can go to paradise later. Now you really should return to your life on earth. Continue with your tasks and make us all proud of you, please. And there is one secret, I can tell you, that is worth to return for. If you do not, you will never know about it", the guardian angel said. "The best is yet to come. Have a little faith, Aiden. If you do not return soon, I will get the angel of death to take you home, I promise you that. Think about it and feel it."

Orla

A couple of days later, when Aiden had recovered from his deadly wounds, and regained his consciousness, he was asked by Ide, what had happened from his point of view, while he was considered to be dead.

"Well, that was so strange, Ide. I thought I was dead, and I saw the angel of death, again, and he took me through the light-tunnel to the other side. It was so beautiful there and there was so much love, it was overwhelming. I really wanted to stay there when the angel said, I would have to return. And then he brought me back to the entrance of the light-tunnel. Somehow, on the other side over there, that felt even more real than this side here. Can you believe that, Ide?", Aiden said.

"To some extent, yes. It is only, the longer you are here again, the more you will find these impressions stepping back into your inner memories, they fade again. But how was it even possible for you to return? Usually, once a soul has gone completely through the tunnel, there is no return, as far as I know", Ide wanted to know from Aiden.

"Yes, that was so strange, Ide", Aiden started to explain. "The angel of death told me, he had to cut the silver ribbon, that connects the physical body with our astral body, so that I would really die. But he did not cut it and so it was possible for me to return and rejoin my astral body with the physical body. You know, what I believe, Ide? There is still a lot for us to explore, such a lot! And I am so happy that I got the chance to continue my journey with all of you here at the school!", Aiden said with tears in his eyes.

Ide gave him a long hug and then said to him: "Yes, it is so good to have you back, but first you need to rest a few more days or weeks until you fully have recovered. Then – and only then – we might consider taking you again with us for new adventures!", Ide said with a smile.

"Of course, my dear!", Aiden replied, teasing Ide.

Aiden should regret his unrefracting remark faster than he liked, as Donal stepped into the room with a young lady in his company.

"Finally,", Donal said to the young woman, "this is Ide. She is most talented to communicate with spiritual entities like fairies and elves. She can see these beautiful beings and she talks with them, like they were one of us. You will surely find that interesting, I believe." And after a short pause, Donal continued: "And this young man is Aiden. He came back from an adventure, deadly wounded, a couple of days ago. He is one of our students at the school." Then Donal turned to Ide and Aiden and introduced the young lady to them: "Ide, Aiden, this young woman is Orla. She came here to Galway with her family and she is profoundly educated in the art of astrology. There is no doubt that our school will deeply benefit from her knowledge in this area, I believe", Donal concluded.

Aiden's mouth stood open as he had seen the face of this young lady. She looked exactly like the woman he was married to in his previous life in Afghanistan. He could not say a word while his heart was beating so strongly, that he felt his pulse in every cell of his body. When Orla touched his hand in greeting, Aiden felt like he was directly hit by a flash from the sky.

And the journey of these souls will continue

…as it always has been…

About the book and how it was created

The idea to write a novel about re-incarnation and magic education was born quite some years ago. It took me quite some time to create the basic idea of the story, which should contain several lives of the main character.

One important item was the creation of the characters of the story itself. How can you imagine several different characters and keep them authentic? My approach to this was to imagine, who could play each character, if the story would be taken for the creation of a movie. I searched pictures of actors and actresses I could assign for the specific roles. Once you have faces to your characters, it is easy to imagine, how they would behave. Second part for the creation of the characters was to imagine real persons, that I had met in my life and in who's activities I had been involved. This was specifically helpful for the villains and the bad characters in the story. It is incredibly helpful to write about their behavior if these real people did something bad or unpleasant to yourself. It is, I would say, a kind of positive psychotherapy and you can pay these people back everything, they did to you in your real life. You can let them fall into the dirt, you can do all kinds of things to them and you can make them stupid, greedy, ugly and like idiots. That releases a lot of bad energy from yourself into the character of a villain, who can benefit from that, for the sake of the story. It is a win-win situation and should one of these real people one day read the book and maybe realize, that he or she is the basis for the villain's character, maybe, that helps them to understand how ugly their behavior towards other people was or still is.

To develop a good story, it is inevitable, that you learn about how to create a story. What is important, how do you describe and progress with the storyline, how do you catch the reader's interest and keep it? It is helpful to read and learn as much as possible as your natural talent (if you have one) can truly benefit from the knowledge of others, who have written stories before you.

Then a basic story was developed, with chapters and ideas, what would happen and who should do what in the story. When you start writing, only a skeleton of these ideas will survive. The more the story comes to life itself, the more things will develop as you write. That is quite surprising and leads to story-changes that you do not foresee. And if you are in the flow, if words come down naturally, the story may also benefit from the freedom to grow, as it wants. This is true inspiration and maybe it is something, that comes from a higher spiritual level. If the story benefits from that, it is fine.

Then – and I do not really know why that was so – something in me wanted, that I write the novel in English, not in German. My natural language is German, but I always liked it to talk in English. Whenever I watch a movie, I prefer to watch it in its natural language, be it English or French. Sure, I still have my difficulties to understand everything. First, I started to watch the movies in German, then a second time in English. Today, I have reached a level that I avoid the German version as it sounds too artificial and unnatural, I only watch movies in English if that is their original language. That helps improve your language skills, indeed. So, I loved the idea to write the novel in English.

That has a couple of beneficial side-effects. First thing is: I only use words, that I know. That keeps the language simple and many people should be able to understand, what is written down as the story. Second benefit is, when I use Google translator to create the German version of the book, I fully understand the translated version and recognize every piece of information, that was not translated in the way, I wanted it to be told. When the German translation was strange, that could be that Google translator did not exactly do, what I expected. Then I simply wrote it in new words. Or – it might have been, that I had used wrong wording in the English version myself – due to the fact, that my English is not perfect and I still make mistakes, when I try to express, what I want to say.

Seeing a bad German translation, because the English original version was written with the wrong words, helped me in many chapters to improve the English writing too. Would I have written the story in German language first and had then used Google translator to get an English version, it might have been, that it had lots of words, that I am not familiar with or that phrases were translated in a way, that were not meant this way and I would not recognize that, as I would not fully understand it. So, finally I would say, the approach to write the book in a foreign language was a very good decision for me and I have learned quite some new English words too, at those points in the story, where I wanted to write something specific, where I could not find the right words by myself.

On the other hand – it might be the case, that the English text does not always sound perfect to a natural English-speaking person. I confidently believe, the readers will have quite some understanding for that, once they know, how the text was created and that I simply could not do it better. The German version also sounds strange at many points of the story. Well, I accept this under the premise, that the text was translated from English to German. Had it been written in German first, then the German version would have had a benefit. Well then – to me it was much more fun to do it the other way round and I highly appreciate Google translator's capabilities to convert the story into a German book, honestly. I also played with the thought to announce "Google Translator" as co-writer for the German version of the book.

Could be, that it would have been the first time, that "Google Translator" would have been named as an author of a book.

Overall – and that is the most important message – it was such a pleasure to me, to write this book. I had so many situations, where I really had to laugh because of some things or phrases in the text, which I myself had not expected to flow into the creative process of the writing of the story.

One day I had an unpleasant phone call from an unpleasant real person I had to deal with. It was a great pleasure and a real joy to transform the message of this call into the storyline at the same day, just a couple of hours later. I strongly believe, the readers will feel the joy, that was transformed into the words of the text too. And for that, even if bad things are happening in your personal life, these can be used and transformed to something beneficial and good.

After I decided to start working on this book, I was open for inspiration that came to me in many ways. If you have an open mind, if you try to learn from all you observe, if you then combine it with your personal essence, your thoughts, your creativity, you can give back a lot to the people in this world, I believe. You decide every day, if you want to do the right things, the good things, or if you fight against others. Karma is the judge for everything we do. We are allowed and we are free to do what we want. Finally, we will be judged by our actions. Our own personal karma will take care, that we understand to differentiate, what is good and what is not. If others feel good about what you do, then it will be good for you too. If others are hurt by your actions, you might consider doing it better next time. We all are making mistakes. We are here to learn. It is always our personal journey. And it is totally okay, if we correct ourselves, when we have learned something from our actions or from our life.

What I have learned from the writing of this book is, that it is so important, that we human beings use our lifetime for things, that make ourselves happy. All that laughter I got back, while I was writing this book, has an incredible worth to me and had a lasting positive effect to my mental condition, I feel.

It is so important that you enjoy your life, live for something good, give the world something back for the positive welcome we all get every day. Nature is supporting us, as good as possible. We are born with empty hands; our relatives take care of us. If our karma allows us to get rewarded positively, we may have a wonderful and good life on this planet earth. When we leave, we go with empty hands. All those things we call our own between our birth and our death can be considered as gifts from our life to us. Can you see, how rich we truly are? And all our experiences, our feelings, all memories – we are allowed to take them with us, carried by our immortal soul for eternity. Isn't that great?

One more thought: As I was open for inspiration from others, I learned a lot from people like Sylvester Stallone and a couple of screenwriters, or people like Stan Lee or J. J. Abrams, by watching their interviews. And one thing, I have remembered is: "Always try, that the next book gets better, than the last one." It is so important, I think, that we always try to give our best, it is important to find an end, to release our projects at a given point in time, so that others can have a look on it, finally. And when we have released a book or any other creation into the public, we will also make our own judgement about the quality of it. And, for me, it is quite normal, that I always find critical thoughts about these finished projects, that I think I could have done them better.

And now the point is: If you do not learn, to let things go, as they are, you will never be content. The better approach is to let go and then simply try, to make it better next time. That really drives us into improvement with an open mind. It is okay, to not be perfect, as it is most important to start, to take action, to begin with a project, whatever it is. Let's just do it.

I have experienced a couple of situations, where I have seen, that women with an impressive talent had not found the courage, to do something with it. They always gave away their chances to a man first, before they found the courage to simply do it by themselves. I can only say: If you are a woman, and you are insecure if you can do something, or if you should do something, if you need an additional education and more and more until you finally would maybe feel prepared to take action – let it go.

If you think you would like to do something creative, something, that is important to you, your feelings, your soul, then do it! Do it now. Do not wait for better times or for the eternity to be better prepared. All you need is to do the step, with courage and now. Don't give away your potential, don't waste or hide it, don't give up your chances. Take care of yourself, take all your courage and then do it, whatever makes you happy! As long, as it helps to make other people happy too, and as long as you can expect positive reward from your karma, it will be fine. And even if it goes wrong – it will make you better, as you learn from your experience. What drives us, is our feeling, the joy that comes naturally, when we do things, that we like, that fill us with joy. Do not let anyone slow you down. Do not let anyone judge on you. Your own judgement should be the hardest and cruelest you can imagine. Let the others talk. Then do, what makes you happy. It is your life, primarily!

If this book and the story in it did entertain you and if you could take some positive messages out for yourself, it has completely fulfilled its purpose.

Thank you all for your interest and for giving the book a chance, and for spending your time with it.

Stay safe, stay healthy and keep your karma clean!

With all best wishes to every single one of you, thank you!

Yours sincerely,

Pearly Scott

P.S.: In the first release of the English version of this book, unfortunately my thanks to pixabay user "RedHeadsRule", Gloria Williams, for the cover picture was missing, which is absolutely essential to be expressed from my side.

@ Gloria Williams:

Dear Gloria Williams,
Your image of the flames, which are building a heart of fire, is so beautiful, that it was clear to me, that it is the perfect cover picture for this book. As Aiden, one of the main characters in it, practices fire magic and explores his feelings, you created the ideal symbol for the whole story. I am thankful for the possibility to use your creation for this book and want to express my deep gratitude and best wishes to you. Thank you very much!

You can break a stick
in two pieces
in a second,
but it takes years
to grow a new one
for you.

Please remember that,
when you try to act
out of an impulse.